She couldn't help but wonder what made him so scared of letting people into his life.

She might not be ready to settle down, but she had close relationships. From what she could tell of Nick, he kept everyone at an arm's length. "We should probably get going soon." She smiled. "I know you'd hate to miss the opening."

He chuckled. "You're right about that." He flagged down the waitress and pulled out his wallet.

Suzanne reached for her purse. She might've let him pay for the barbecue the other night, but dinner at the Majestic Grille was in a different league.

"Put your purse away. This is my treat." He winked. "And I won't even try and put the moves on you at the end of the night; I promise."

She laughed. "Thanks."

He placed some cash on the table and guided her out of the restaurant.

The feel of his hand on the small of her back sent delicious shivers up her spine. There was just something about him.... She would have to be very careful not to fall under his spell. She'd had her heart broken once a long time ago.

And it was not an experience she intended to repeat.

ANNALISA DAUGHETY, a graduate of Freed-Hardeman University, writes contemporary fiction set in historic locations. Annalisa lives in Arkansas with two spoiled dogs and is hard at work on her next book. She loves to connect with her readers through social media sites like Facebook and Twitter. More information about Annalisa can be found at her website, www.annalisadaughety.com.

All Shook Up

Annalisa Daughety

Heartsong Presents

I'm blessed beyond measure by a wonderfully supportive family and friends who are quick to offer prayers and encouragement. I'm especially grateful to my mom, Vicky Daughety. Thanks for always being my first reader. I couldn't do it without you!

A note from the Author:
I love to hear from my readers! You may correspond with me by writing:

Annalisa Daughety
Author Relations
P.O. Box 9048
Buffalo, NY 14240-9048

ISBN-13: 978-0-373-48600-7

ALL SHOOK UP

This edition issued by special arrangement with Barbour Publishing, Inc., 1810 Barbour Drive, Uhrichsville, Ohio, U.S.A.

Printed in the U.S.A.

one

Suzanne Simpson bolted toward her gate at Atlanta's Hartsfield-Jackson International Airport, sidestepping a group of texting teens and a woman wearing three-inch heels. *What kind of person travels in shoes like that?* Suzanne wasn't sure she wanted to know the answer.

She slowed down as she reached her gate in Concourse C and struggled to catch her breath. It never failed. Whenever she flew through Atlanta, her connecting flight inevitably boarded in a different concourse than her arriving flight. Which meant a mad dash through one of the largest airports in the country. At least she had the wisdom to wear flats when she traveled.

"Final boarding for Delta flight sixteen fifty-eight," a voice over the loudspeaker declared. The flight was the last one out of Atlanta tonight. If she didn't make it, she'd be stuck until morning. And with the work week that loomed ahead, she knew she couldn't afford to sleep in the airport tonight.

Suzanne cast a woeful glance at the restroom and fished her boarding pass out of her bag. She held it out as she rushed to the gate.

The attendant quickly scanned her pass and ushered her through the door.

Lord, be with me, and get me home safely. Guide the pilot's actions, and be with all those involved in the operation of the airplane. Every flight, no matter what, Suzanne prayed as she walked down the jet bridge to board the aircraft. It calmed her down. Even though she flew frequently, a fear of flying still lingered.

The flight attendant waiting at the doorway frowned. "You're the last passenger," the woman said. "Please take your seat quickly."

"Sorry. My last flight was late. I got here as soon as I could." Suzanne's words seemed to placate the crew member. Suzanne hoisted her bag over her shoulder and hurried down the aisle to her seat. She grinned at a group of men in first class who were dressed like Elvis. She didn't have to wonder where they were headed.

She stopped at her seat and glanced up at the numbers overhead to make sure she had the right one. Yep. And someone already occupied it. "Excuse me, sir?" she asked. A quick glance told her the flight attendant was glowering at her from the front of the plane.

The man in her seat never looked up. He had his eyes closed and appeared to be listening to an MP3 player.

Suzanne sighed. She hated the aisle seat. If a window seat wasn't available when she booked a trip, she chose another flight. *This is not my day.* She crumpled into the empty aisle seat and tucked her bag underneath the seat in front of her. She hadn't had time to charge her iPhone at the gate as she'd planned, so she couldn't even listen to music on the flight. She tilted her head back against the seat and closed her eyes.

And felt someone staring at her.

Her eyes popped open, and the guy next to her quickly looked down.

"You know you're in my seat," she said loudly.

No response.

"You're in my seat," she said in a louder voice. She was probably coming across as bratty, but she didn't care. She'd had a bad weekend. Breaking up with someone was never easy, especially when it was with a guy as nice as Jeremy. And now, all she wanted was to be able to lean her head against the window and sleep for the next hour.

Except that this guy wouldn't move. Or acknowledge her. This guy with a faded Braves hat that he wore so low she wasn't totally sure he even had eyes. He reminded her of all the frat boys from college she'd worked hard to ignore.

The flight attendant gave out last-minute safety instructions at the front of the aircraft. Even though Suzanne had heard them a million times, she watched the demonstration. Secure your own oxygen first, use your seat cushion as a flotation device, and the closest exit might be behind you. . . . None of those tips ever reassured her. Flying might be faster, but Suzanne was pretty sure she aged ten years with each trip she took. And now that she was nearing thirty, she'd just as soon stop that process. *Next time, I'm driving.*

Suzanne took a deep breath as the plane taxied down the runway. *Please keep us safe, Lord.* One more prayer wouldn't hurt. The plane lifted into the air, and Suzanne gripped the armrest.

Ten minutes later, they'd reached their cruising altitude. Suzanne relaxed her grip and looked around. She smiled at a toddler two seats up. *See, it's fine. Everything is fine.*

The overhead speakers crackled to life. "Welcome aboard Delta flight sixteen fifty-eight; this is your captain speaking. On behalf of our crew, thanks for choosing to fly with us tonight. There are thunderstorms ahead, so please remain seated with your seat belts fastened. We might experience a bit of turbulence as we pass over the unstable air mass, but it's nothing to be concerned about. Sit back and enjoy your flight."

Suzanne bit her lip. Thunderstorms were the worst. And this plane wasn't exactly huge. One lightning strike and they'd probably wind up somewhere in the wilderness that was Mississippi. She focused on her breathing to calm herself down.

"Nervous flyer, huh?" A male voice next to her asked.

She glanced up and met the brown eyes of the guy who'd stolen her seat. *So you do have eyes under that hat.* His grin told her he felt no remorse for his travel faux pas. "I guess you could say that."

He rifled through his backpack and pulled out a pack of gum and a Dean Koontz novel. It wasn't every day she came across a guy who liked to read. And even if he'd broken the airplane etiquette rules, she had to admit he had nice eyes. And a great smile.

"How about you? Flying doesn't make you nervous?" she asked, watching as he popped a piece of gum in his mouth then held out the package to her. She plucked a stick of gum from the package.

He shook his head. "Nope. I figure if it's my time to go, it's my time to go." He grinned. "No sense worrying about something I can't control, right?"

Suzanne flashed him a tiny smile. He sounded an awful lot like her grandpa. "Good philosophy, I guess."

"'Therefore do not worry about tomorrow, for tomorrow will worry about itself. Each day has enough trouble of its own,'" he quoted with a grin. "Matthew 6:34."

A book-reading, Bible-quoting cutie. Maybe she could

overlook his penchant for stealing window seats. She offered him an encouraging grin.

"So is Memphis your final destination?" he asked.

She nodded. "Yes. How about you?"

"Me, too." He grinned and held out a hand. "Sorry, I forgot my manners. I'm Nick Taggart."

She shook his outstretched hand. "Suzanne Simpson." She appreciated his firm grip. Grandpa used to say that you could tell a lot about a man by the way he shook hands. If that was true, she'd have to surmise that Nick Taggart brimmed with confidence.

"Well, Suzanne, are you Memphis-bound for business or pleasure?"

Making airplane small talk was definitely not on Suzanne's list of favorites, but Nick's good looks could turn her into a fan. "Actually neither." She smiled. "I live there."

A shadow crossed his face. "I see."

The plane lurched, and Suzanne gripped the armrest. She peered ahead and glimpsed the flight attendant swaying as she tried to make her way to a seat. The plane dropped suddenly, along with Suzanne's stomach. It might be a fun feeling on a roller coaster, but thousands of feet in the air, it induced panic.

Suzanne closed her eyes and held on tightly.

❧

Nick Taggart studied the woman beside him out of the corner of his eye. She kept such a tight grip on the armrest, it probably had a dent from her fingers. Her closed eyes gave him license to admire her profile. Long lashes, a slightly upturned nose, and full lips. She was definitely cute. No. She was beautiful, but in an unassuming way. Like she didn't try too hard. Her blond hair was shorter than most of the girls he was attracted to, but it suited her. He liked the way the ends flipped up. Made her seem kind of unpredictable.

As the plane jerked, Suzanne opened her eyes and caught him staring. "Do you mind?" she asked.

He fought back a grin. "Sorry. I was checking to see if you're okay. I'd just as soon not get thrown up on or anything."

She glared at him with eyes the color of the Mediterranean. "I'm not sick. A little on edge maybe, but not sick."

Nick chuckled. "I thought we established that there was no point in worrying."

"I'm not worrying, just nervous." She scowled. "You're in my seat, you know. If the plane goes down, they probably won't be able to identify me because some man is in 16A."

He groaned. "I'm sorry. I always get the window seat. I must not have paid attention." He gazed into her narrowed eyes. "Honestly. My bad."

Her face relaxed. "That's fine. I was a little late boarding. Besides, your hogging the window seat means I don't feel bad about hogging the armrest." She inhaled sharply as the plane dropped again.

Nick leaned closer to her. So close he could smell her perfume. Or shampoo. Whatever it was, it smelled like honeysuckle. "How about we play a little game? Take your mind off the storm."

She eyed him suspiciously. "I don't make it a practice to play games with strangers, but considering we could soon be plummeting to the ground, I'll make an exception."

He shook his head. "Okay. Twenty questions. Me first." He adjusted his baseball cap. "Are you a cat person or a dog person?"

"Dog. Cats hate me for some reason. I have a dog named Charlie though, and I can't wait to see him if we ever get off of this plane." She regarded him for a long minute. "My turn. Is your favorite holiday Christmas or Thanksgiving?"

"Neither. My favorite holiday is the Fourth of July." He didn't want to go into details, but he wasn't exactly a brimming-with-holiday-spirit kind of guy. In fact, a few years ago he'd started taking tropical vacations during the holiday season. An indulgent vacation made him feel less alone and gave him something to look forward to as everyone else was all caught up in happy memories of family get-togethers and caroling in the snow.

Suzanne looked at him with wide eyes. "Really? Wow. I just figured. . . Well I thought most people would choose one or the other."

Nick shrugged. "I'm not most people."

"Clearly." She grinned.

"Ladies and gentlemen, we're making our initial descent into Memphis. Attendants, please prepare the cabin for landing."

Nick smiled at Suzanne. "How about that? We're almost there and no plummeting."

"Yet." She quirked her mouth into a grin. "Landing *is* the most dangerous part."

He chuckled. "Why am I not surprised to hear you say that?"

"Just keeping it real."

Ten minutes later they were on the ground. Suzanne stood and peered down at Nick. "The upside to the aisle seat—I get to deplane first." She shot him a sassy grin and started down the aisle.

He laughed. He liked the way she didn't cut him any

slack. He grabbed his backpack and followed her toward the terminal. He headed toward baggage claim just steps behind Suzanne. She'd joined up with a group of Elvis impersonators, and they were clearly trying to impress her. The smell of barbecue hung thick in the air. Even at the airport, the city's delicacy was all around him.

Hello again, Memphis. It's been awhile. But I'm sure you're still the same.

two

Suzanne stood at baggage claim, waiting impatiently for her bag to appear on the conveyor belt. She scanned the crowd to see if Nick Taggart was around. She hadn't asked him why he'd come to Memphis, but she guessed business. He struck her as one of those party-boy business types who saw work travel as the chance to sample the best restaurants on the company dime and flirt with girls on planes. And probably wherever else he went. She hadn't noticed a wedding ring, but experience told her that meant nothing.

"So we'll see you at some point this week, right?" an older man asked, lumbering up alongside her. His white Elvis jumpsuit was missing a few rhinestones, and his plump belly was more reminiscent of Elvis's later years than the prime of his youth. He grinned. "I'm George. We met as we exited the plane."

She nodded. "I'll be there all week. I hope you and your friends enjoy the city."

"Oh, we will. We're headed to Heartbreak Hotel now, and tomorrow we're going to Neely's to eat barbecue with all the fixin's." He grinned. "Memphis does it a little different than we're used to in Texas, you know."

Suzanne smiled. "Yes, sir. But I know better than to debate you about who does it better." Living in a barbecue-centric town meant an ongoing debate about what style was best. As far as Suzanne was concerned, Memphis style beat Texas or the Carolinas any day of the week.

George chuckled. "I wouldn't dream of it. We'll call it a draw." He shot her a wink and grabbed a bag from the conveyer.

Suzanne eyed his suitcase, wondering if it was full of Elvis-themed attire or if George and his buddies had dressed up just for the enjoyment of their fellow air travelers. "Take care," she called as he joined his friends and walked out the sliding doors to the parking lot.

"Do you attract crazies everywhere you go?" Nick Taggart asked from behind her.

She whirled to face him. "Obviously. I mean, you're next to me again, aren't you?"

Nick chuckled. "Touché." He raised his hands up in surrender. "I meant those old Elvis wannabes. What's the deal with them?"

Suzanne spotted her bag coming around the belt. She leaned forward to snatch it, but Nick's strong hands scooped it up and gently put it on the ground. "You must not have read your Memphis guidebook before you picked this week to travel," she teased.

He furrowed his brow. "What's this week?"

Suzanne smirked as her eyes twinkled. "Welcome to Elvis Week. All Elvis, all week long."

He groaned. "Between that and the barbecue smell wafting around, it's like I'm stuck inside of a Memphis cliché." He shook his head. "So I guess Elvis fans will be out in full force, huh?"

"Yep. From every country around the world. You should

hang out at Graceland if you want the full effect." She grinned.

"Ugh. What kind of person would want to spend time at such a kitschy place?" He laughed.

Suzanne frowned. "I work there." She locked eyes with him, daring him to continue poking fun.

He swallowed. "Oh. Wow. Sorry." He tugged at his baseball hat. "What do you do there?"

"Event planning. Specifically weddings. There's a chapel on the grounds." Suzanne could admit to herself that it might not be her dream position, but she'd never tell Nick. Especially given the obvious disdain on his face.

Nick grabbed a large suitcase from the conveyer. "Sounds like fun." The tone of his voice told her that he thought otherwise.

"It is." She gave him a tiny smile and pulled up the suitcase handle. "I'd better go. It's late. Nice to meet you, Nick. Enjoy Memphis." Before he had time to respond, she stepped out the double doors and to the crosswalk. The August humidity spread over her like a warm blanket. Almost eleven and it was still miserably hot. She paused at the crosswalk and tried to remember which lot she'd parked in. She should've written it down but had been in such a hurry on Friday afternoon that she hadn't given it much attention.

"Suzanne," Nick called. "Wait." He jogged over to her. "Um. Listen. Do you have a card or something? Because now that I know what you do, I might be able to use your services."

She eyed him warily. He wanted to plan a wedding? At Graceland? *Stop judging. He might have an Elvis-loving fiancée back home. Wherever that is.* "Sure." She reached into her purse and pulled out a business card. "Here you go."

Nick took the card and shoved it in his pocket. "Thanks." He shifted from one foot to the other, clearly uncomfortable. "Well it was nice to meet you, Suzanne. I'll be in touch soon."

Sure you will. She waved and started off toward a row of cars, hoping she looked like she knew where she was going.

❧

Nick watched her walk away. How lame was he? He was the last person in the world who needed a wedding planner. Especially one who specialized in the ultimate Memphis wedding. He walked back to where he'd left his suitcase, thankful it was still there.

He rolled his suitcase toward the long row of waiting taxicabs. Even though his grandmother had tried to arrange for someone pick him up, he'd insisted on taking a cab. Returning to Memphis after ten years was awkward enough without having to make nice with some distant cousin or a well-meaning family friend. He shoved his bag into the first cab he came to and climbed inside. "I'm headed to Germantown," he said. He gave the driver the address, and the older man raised an eyebrow.

"Nice neighborhood," the man observed as he pulled the car away from the airport and merged onto 240.

Nick shrugged. "I haven't been back in years." The upscale area of town where his grandmother lived had always been and would always be desirable. Some things never changed, no matter how much time passed. He leaned back and watched familiar sights pass by. The driver exited onto Poplar Avenue, and Nick couldn't help but grin. He wasn't far from where he'd attended high school. The elite boys' prep school had been the same one his dad had attended. Those had been some happy days, right up until his junior year when his whole world fell apart.

A few things were different—maybe a couple more Starbucks—but for the most part the city looked like it had when he left. And as much as he tried, there were some things he just couldn't forget.

Even after ten years, Nick still had nightmares about Memphis. It didn't matter if he was on the other side of the world, he couldn't get away from this town. The past filled his dreams: the people he'd left behind—and those who'd left him—the smell of barbecue during the annual barbecue festival, the sound of the blues that drifted out of any number of places along Beale Street, and the way his mother laughed with him when she'd tuck him in at night.

Some might say those memories were the stuff sweet dreams were made of, but they held Nick hostage. And now that he was back—back in this city that had never loosened her hold on him no matter how many miles he put in between—he wasn't sure how he would deal with the days to come.

"Here we are, sir." The cab driver pulled into the driveway of Grandmother's expansive two-story home. Nick handed him some bills. "Keep the change." He hoisted his suitcase from the car and walked slowly to the door. He pulled his key ring out of his pocket and stuck a key in the lock. Ten years and it still fit. *Glad something still fits in here, because I sure don't.*

The alarm beeped as he entered the dark room, and he quickly punched in the code. His birthday. It had been the alarm code for as long as there'd been an alarm. He closed the door and flipped on the light. The house felt empty without his grandmother, despite the welcoming decor.

The cushy couch beckoned him, and Nick didn't even bother going upstairs to the room that had once been his. He'd camp out here. Besides, it was almost midnight, and tomorrow would be a long day full of hospital waiting rooms and unfamiliar medical terms. He sure didn't want to suffer the inevitable sleepless night that sleeping in his old room, surrounded by tangible memories of the past, would bring. *The couch it is.*

He sat on the couch and emptied the contents of his pockets onto the coffee table. Along with the usual change and lint was Suzanne Simpson's business card. Nick picked it up and stared at it for a long moment. He wasn't planning to be in town for long, which would keep things from going too far or getting too complicated. He certainly didn't want any strings to tie him down. But Suzanne, with her quick wit and easy smile, could be a welcome distraction from the ghosts sure to be haunting every corner in the city. And then in a few weeks, he'd be on to his next destination. *Perfect.* He tapped his finger against the card.

Perhaps he'd call her for a wedding consultation. Just for fun.

And maybe he'd even find his next story waiting at the gates of Graceland.

three

Suzanne clipped the leash on Charlie and helped him out of her white Pathfinder. "You ready for a walk?" she cooed. She glanced around the parking lot at Sea Isle Park. There were a lot of cars, but she didn't spot the one she was looking for. Screams from a soccer game reached her ears. The park was one of her favorite things about her neighborhood in East Memphis. Situated next to an elementary school, it offered a walking track, a baseball field, playground equipment, and plenty of green space. Truly something for everyone.

Charlie pulled against his leash, ready to go. Suzanne had rescued him from the pound when he was a tiny puppy. That had been more than ten years ago, and the boxer mix was still going strong. He had a little bit of gray in his reddish-brown hair, but he could still run as fast as a puppy. At least for one lap. "Hang on a minute, boy." She reached down and scratched behind his ears.

A black BMW screeched into the parking lot and jerked to a stop. "Sorry I'm late," Emily Madden said, climbing out of the vehicle. "Hope you weren't waiting long." Even wearing exercise clothes, no makeup, and her long, red hair in a ponytail, Emily still managed to look like a supermodel.

Suzanne grinned. "Not a problem. Work was crazy today, and I just pulled into the parking lot a couple of minutes before you."

They headed toward the walking track.

"Want to walk one lap before we jog?" Suzanne asked.

Emily nodded. "Works for me. I haven't been to the gym at all lately, so let's just say I'm behind on my training." They'd signed up to run in the St. Jude half-marathon that took place each December in downtown Memphis but were having trouble fitting in training time.

"Me, too. I'm kind of thinking maybe we should do the 5K that day instead of the half." Suzanne grinned. "We'll still be doing something for a good cause, but maybe we won't faint in the middle of Beale Street."

Emily laughed. "Yeah, that wouldn't look very good for me. I should probably keep my fainting to a minimum considering so many of my colleagues will be there." Emily worked as a nurse at St. Jude Children's Research Hospital where she treated children from all over the country who had cancer. The hospital never turned away families because of their inability to pay. The race each year was one of many fundraisers across the country that benefited the hospital.

"I guess not." Suzanne kept a tight grip on Charlie's leash as they neared a series of newly planted trees. As he got older, he wanted to do more sniffing and less walking and had a bad habit of winding himself around trees if Suzanne wasn't paying close attention.

"So. . .tell me how it went this weekend. Was Jeremy-the-Accountant totally heartbroken?" Emily chuckled. Suzanne always labeled her suitors by their jobs, much to the amusement of her friends.

Suzanne rolled her eyes. "Not really. I gave him my usual speech about how I didn't see whatever was between us being a long-term thing." She shrugged. "You know the drill."

Emily shook her head. "You never cease to amaze me. I mean, aren't you afraid that someday you're going to throw away a perfectly good guy? What if you've already missed out on Mr. Right because you didn't want to get tied down?"

Suzanne would readily admit that she was a commitment-phobe. She never stuck with anything—or anyone—very long. The thought of being locked into something for the long haul made her queasy. It was probably part of the reason why she'd never bought a home of her own. She'd moved in and out of more rental houses than she could even count, always searching for something nicer and for a better price. Yes, she was certainly not one to settle down. "I'm not afraid of missing Mr. Right because, honestly, I don't think he exists."

❧

Nick stood outside his grandmother's hospital room clutching a bouquet of flowers he'd gotten at the gift shop. He took a deep breath and rapped on the door.

"Come in," Grandmother called. She still sounded the same.

Nick pasted a smile on his face and stepped inside. "Hey there, beautiful," he said.

She chuckled. "Those lines might work on the younger ladies, but I've been around the block long enough to know better. Don't think you can sweet-talk me and give me flowers to make up for your long absence." She waved him over.

He set the flowers on the table and walked over to her bed. She looked just like she had when he was growing up. Maybe a few more wrinkles, but her blue eyes shone as bright as ever. She wasn't letting a stay in the hospital keep her from having her lipstick on and her hair fixed. Grandmother had always been a bit of a Southern belle.

"Well don't just stand there looking at me; come here and hug my neck."

Nick grinned and embraced her frail frame. "How are you feeling?"

"I'm ready to go home."

He chuckled. "You haven't even had your surgery yet."

She raised an eyebrow. "I know. That's the point." She sighed. "I'm not especially looking forward to being opened up on an operating table. After all, the only time I've ever even been in the hospital was when I delivered your father." She smiled. "I never expected to be nearly eighty and have to go in for heart surgery."

Nick reached out and took her hand. "Congestive heart failure is nothing to mess around with. If the doctor thinks bypass surgery will help you, then I'm glad you're doing it."

Grandmother shook her head. "There are a lot of things that can go wrong, Nicholas. In a patient my age, especially." She patted the bed. "Sit down."

Nick carefully sat down next to her. "It will go fine. Everything will be fine." It had to. She was all he had left.

"I haven't seen you in four years, not since I flew up to Boston to visit. Where are you living now? The last time we talked you were thinking about moving. Again."

He hung his head. This woman had done so much for him. And he hadn't seen or talked to her in so long. They e-mailed, but less and less frequently it seemed. "I'm sort of between places right now. I'm not sure where I want to go next."

She clucked her tongue. "New York, Boston, Miami, Los Angeles..." She ticked his former cities off on her hand. "And

I know there are more that I'm leaving out." She frowned at him, and the wrinkles next to her mouth grew more pronounced. "You can't run forever, you know."

"I'm not running. Just exploring." Nick didn't stay in one place long enough to form many attachments. Not to the people or to the place. He figured he got the best of what each city had to offer and then was off on another adventure.

"You're never going to be happy until you make a real home for yourself. Put down some roots." She clasped his hand. "You might be surprised at how much you like that lifestyle."

He grinned. "I happen to like the lifestyle I have. Very much. Don't worry about me."

Grandmother pursed her lips but didn't chide him anymore. "I can't help but worry some. That's what grandmothers do." Her lips turned upward into a smile. "It's so good to see you. I hope you'll stick around through the holidays. I know so many of your old friends would love to see you."

He grimaced. No way was he staying here for months. Weeks, tops. Just long enough to make sure Grandmother recovered and was back on her feet. It was the least he could do. Then he'd hop a plane out of here. Maybe he'd spend some time down on the coast of Mexico. Baja might be a nice place to spend the holidays. "We'll see." He leaned down and kissed her cheek. "Now get some rest."

four

Suzanne couldn't believe it was already Elvis Week. This was the third year she'd worked at Graceland, and the excitement of the crowds never ceased to amaze her. And neither did the August humidity. She stood in the middle of Graceland Plaza and looked around at the throngs of people. Grabbing a quick bite was out of the question today. There were three restaurants on site, but Suzanne didn't even have to see them to know they overflowed with tourists.

She sighed and sat down on a bench. She hadn't quite recovered from being in Atlanta all weekend. She should've known better than to book the last flight out on Sunday night. But it had saved her a couple hundred dollars, and she needed to cut corners wherever she could. Yesterday had been a blur, trying to pull together last-minute details at work and then meeting Emily for a run. This was the first moment she'd stopped moving in what seemed like days.

Suzanne watched the activity around her and enjoyed catching snippets of different languages as people strolled by. It made her feel like she was in Europe again, where multiple languages were common. She'd backpacked there during college and still considered it one of her fondest memories even though it had been more than eight years ago.

Her buzzing cell phone ended her stroll down memory lane. "This is Suzanne; how can I help you?" Last year she'd started using the same cell phone for work and for personal use because she hated juggling two. But the downside was that she was always plugged in to work, even on breaks or after hours. Elvis Week was chock full of events, and everyone in her department was on high alert.

"Suzanne as in Suzanne Simpson, nervous flyer?" a male voice said, chuckling.

Nick. She hadn't expected to hear from him. "Well, well. Nick Taggart. Is your business trip not shaping up to be the thrill you expected?" She laughed. "I figured by now you would've tossed my card in favor of someone new." *And someone younger and cuter.*

He cleared his throat. "I'm not actually in town on business."

"I just assumed..." She trailed off. After the way he'd reacted to the Elvis impersonators and the smell of Memphis barbecue that permeated the airport, he certainly hadn't seemed like he was in town for fun. "To what do I owe this pleasure?"

"Actually I was hoping to stop by your office. I'm at Graceland."

She widened her eyes. "No way." So maybe he'd been serious the other night about needing her services. "Where are you exactly?"

"Just got parked. It's a zoo out here."

She laughed. "Told you." She glanced around. The crowd had thinned out some. "I'm on my lunch break right now. Take the walkway that leads to the ticket office. I'll meet you right outside." She rose from her seat and made her way over to the building.

Five minutes later, she spotted him on the covered walkway. Clad in a red polo shirt and khaki shorts, he looked ready for a day on the golf course. His hair was a little longer than she'd expected now that it wasn't covered by a baseball hat. Not too long, but definitely on the shaggy side. It suited him though. He struck her as the kind of man who couldn't be bothered to schedule a haircut.

"Hi there," he said with a grin. His brown eyes had flecks of gold in them that she hadn't noticed the other night.

"Welcome to Graceland." She struck a spokesmodel pose. "These are the shops and restaurants. The mansion is across the street."

"Did you used to work as a tour guide?" he asked with a laugh.

She shook her head. "Nope. But I find myself saying the same things over and over as I answer questions for people planning weddings and events here." She raised an eyebrow at him. "So do you really need a wedding planner?"

Nick shook his head. "Not at this moment in time, but I might someday."

Suzanne regarded him for a moment. She wondered if that meant he had a girlfriend somewhere who he considered a potential fiancée or if his "someday" had just been used generically. But she didn't want to pry. It wasn't any of her business.

"Well then. . . Come sit down, and let me fill you in on the specifics of a Graceland wedding." She motioned toward the plaza.

❧

Nick had been impressed by her the other night on the plane. But today, she blew him away. Suzanne wore a simple, black sleeveless dress and black heels. Her red nail polish caught his eye immediately, followed by how long and trim her legs were. But he felt drawn to her for more than just her looks. Something about her personality captivated him.

"Sorry to barge in on your workday like this." He glanced around. "I've never actually been to Graceland, so I figured this was as good of a time as any to come." The truth was that he hadn't known what to do with himself. Grandmother's surgery had been postponed, and he couldn't just sit at the hospital all day. He'd driven around the city, but it had only left him sad and lonely. *My life sounds like an Elvis song.*

"Don't worry about it. I'm glad to help you however I can." She glanced at her watch. "Although I don't have too much time. I have a meeting in fifteen minutes."

Nick grinned. "You know what? I have a great idea. How about we talk later? Say, over dinner?" He raised his eyebrows. "My treat." Even to his own ears, his invitation sounded suspiciously like a date.

A pink blush spread over Suzanne's cheeks. "Dinner? Oh, I don't know."

"Come on. I'll meet you at your favorite barbecue place."

She chuckled. "Okay. Dinner tonight. But it will have to be kind of early. I have to be at the midnight breakfast that officially kicks off Elvis Week." She grinned. "Unless you'd rather just come to that."

He grinned. "I'm not sure I'm ready for that. Early dinner is fine. Say six?"

"Six o'clock. Central BBQ. Don't be late." She grinned. "And let's go to the one on Central Avenue. It's the original."

Nick had eaten there a lot when he was in high school. The restaurant had been new then. But from one of the articles he'd read in the hospital waiting room that morning, it had clearly become one of Memphis's favorite spots. "I'll meet you outside at six sharp."

"See you then." She flashed him a smile and walked away.

Nick stayed put. He wasn't really in the mood to tour Graceland today after all. He'd forgotten how hot Memphis was in August, and he certainly didn't want to fight the crowds. Besides, scheduling dinner with Suzanne was worth the fee he'd paid to park his car.

He slid into his grandmother's gold Lexus and headed North on Elvis Presley Boulevard toward the interstate. There was one place he wanted to go today. He'd been putting it off, but he knew it was now or never.

Nick merged onto Poplar Avenue and drove for a quarter of a mile. He flipped on his turn signal and turned into the entrance for Memphis Memorial Park, one of the largest cemeteries in the city. The last time he'd visited had been the day of his parents' and brother's funeral, nearly twelve years ago. But he remembered exactly how to get to their final resting place.

After all, he saw it in his dreams almost every night.

five

"You're seriously going to meet the airplane guy?" Emily's voice rose an octave with each word.

Suzanne grinned into the phone. Emily was her most cautious friend. That was probably what made her a good nurse, but it didn't do much for her social life. "Nick's harmless. We're meeting at Central BBQ. You can't get much more public than that."

Emily groaned. "But you know this can't go anywhere. He's just some guy you met on a plane who is probably only in town for a couple of days. Why bother?"

"Because it can't go anywhere. Because he's cute and funny." As far as Suzanne was concerned, agreeing to have dinner with Nick had been a no-brainer. She got to enjoy the company of a handsome, intelligent man without having to worry that he'd expect anything from her.

"We've been friends since undergrad, and yet I still don't understand you sometimes." Emily and Suzanne had started out sharing a room at the University of Memphis before they figured out they worked better as friends than roommates. Suzanne had hated dorm life and moved into an apartment near campus, and Emily had moved into a sorority house, but they'd remained close friends ever since.

Suzanne pulled into the parking lot at Central BBQ. "I'm here. I'll tell you all about it next week when we run. Three miles, right?"

Emily laughed. "Sure. Three miles. Have fun tonight."

Suzanne put the Pathfinder in PARK and cut off the engine. She glanced at herself in the mirror. *Not bad.* She'd had just enough time to run home and let Charlie out before dinner and had taken advantage of that bit of time to touch up her lipstick and hair. She craned her neck to see if Nick was standing at the entrance. He was nowhere to be seen.

A loud tap on her window made her jump. She glanced up to see a beaming Nick standing outside the vehicle. She opened the door. "Sneaky, sneaky. I thought we were meeting at the entrance." They walked slowly toward the restaurant.

"I was. But people kept looking at me funny, so I went back to my car." He grinned. "Besides, I was a little afraid you were going to stand me up."

She returned his smile. "Oh, I never turn down barbecue."

He chuckled and held the door open for her. They joined the line at the counter.

"So you rented a car?"

Nick shook his head. "No. I borrowed one." He met her questioning gaze. "From my grandmother."

Suzanne widened her eyes. "Your grandmother? You didn't mention her the other night on the plane."

He shrugged. "I didn't think I'd ever see you again. I figured there wasn't any point in sharing personal details."

His explanation made sense to Suzanne. She didn't share such information easily either. "So that's what brought you to Memphis? Visiting your grandma?"

Before he could answer, it was their turn to order. Suzanne always got the same thing. "I'll have a pork plate and sweet tea."

Nick smiled at her. "Good choice." He nodded at the man

behind the counter. "I'il have the same." He paid for their meals and grabbed two cups from the cashier. He held one out to her. "Here you go."

"Thanks." She followed him to the self-serve drink station. "I'd be glad to pay for my food. I wasn't really looking for a free meal."

He chuckled. "Nope. This is my treat. I'm happy not to have to eat alone."

She furrowed her brow. "What about your grandmother?" Suzanne filled her cup with ice then sweet tea. "Doesn't she want you to have dinner with her tonight?"

Nick shook his head. "She's in the hospital."

Guilt washed over Suzanne. She'd really read him wrong on the plane. She'd assumed he was in town to sample the food and flirt with the women. Instead he must be here because his grandma was sick. "I'm sorry. I hope she gets better soon."

Nick motioned for her to lead the way to a table. "She's having heart surgery later this week." They sat down at a small table in the corner. The restaurant was nearly at capacity even though it was relatively early on a Tuesday night.

"Wow." Suzanne sipped her tea. "I hope everything turns out okay."

"Thanks." He smiled at her across the table. "The truth of the matter is that I grew up here. I just haven't been back in a decade."

She raised her eyebrows. "Seriously? You're from Memphis?" She'd gotten the impression the other night that he wasn't at all enamored with the city, but she'd never suspected he was a native.

He nodded. "Yeah. But I left after high school and haven't been back since."

"What about your family? They didn't care? Your parents don't mind that you've stayed away for so long?" Her own mother might not win any awards for parenthood, but she'd still be miffed if Suzanne didn't come home for a decade.

He shook his head. "They aren't here now. Just my grandmother."

Suzanne didn't want to keep peppering him with questions. The expression on his face told her that he would rather talk about anything besides his family. She could certainly identify. "Well then welcome back to Memphis. Will you see many old friends while you're here?"

"I haven't really kept in touch with them. But I'm thinking about giving my best friend from childhood a call. We e-mail every now and then. He and his wife live in Collierville. They have a couple of kids I think."

"Number thirty-five," the cashier said over the loudspeaker. "Your order is ready."

"I'll get it." Nick stood and walked over to the pickup window.

He wasn't anything like she'd expected him to be. Her friends would have a field day with that revelation. They were always chiding Suzanne for making snap judgments about people without really getting to know them. Emily said it was because Suzanne was scared she'd meet someone she actually cared about. An accusation Suzanne vehemently denied, but deep down she knew there might be a grain of truth to her friend's claim.

"Here you go," Nick said. He placed two heaping barbecue platters on the table.

"Yum." Suzanne grinned. "It looks great."

Nick nodded. "I haven't been here in ten years, and it smells just like I remember." He placed his napkin in his lap. "Do you mind if I pray?"

She shook her head. "Not at all."

Nick said a quick prayer, asking God to bless their food and the time they spent together.

Suzanne caught his eye when he was finished. One of the drawbacks to her haphazard approach to dating was that many of the guys she went out with weren't Christians. That had never been much of an issue because in each instance, she knew the relationship wasn't going anywhere. But watching Nick live out his faith right in front of her made him even more attractive. "So what do you do, exactly?" she asked.

"I'm a freelancer."

She waited for him to offer more of an explanation, but he remained quiet. "Okay. . . What exactly do you freelance?"

He chuckled. "I write. Mostly articles for magazines, and I provide content for a couple of websites." He shrugged. "I sort of fell into it. I've always loved writing and started out wanting to pen the great American novel. But when I lived in New York, I met a guy who works as a magazine editor, and we became pretty good friends. He had me submit some things to him, and from there, I got more work. It sort of snowballed into a full-time gig."

"I don't mean to keep on with the questions, but where do you live?" Suzanne asked.

A shadow crossed Nick's face. "That's kind of a tricky question."

❧

Nick hated trying to explain his lifestyle to people. Particularly someone like Suzanne. She seemed so normal, so grounded.

She'd never understand. "I'm sort of a vagabond." He grinned, hoping his dimple might distract her from further investigating his personal life.

She frowned.

No such luck. *Guess my charm isn't going to get me anywhere with this one.* "I've lived all over the country since I graduated from college. New York, LA, Boston, Miami. . .even Europe for a little while." Bumming through Italy and Spain had made him feel like Hemingway, bringing an odd mix of happiness and loneliness, but without the acclaimed novel. Or the drinking problem.

"Okay. So you move a lot."

She had no idea the extent to which he went to keep his life free of complications. "Yes. I choose a city with a good public transportation system. I rent a nice apartment downtown that's within walking distance of restaurants and night life." He shrugged. "It's the perfect life."

She drew her brows together. "Are you trying to convince me or yourself?"

"I don't need to convince myself. I move every couple of years after I've gotten to know a city well. I'm kind of considering DC next. Maybe I'll slant my writing toward politics or something."

"Doesn't all that moving kind of hinder your relationships?"

What relationships? "Not at all. I make friends easily." He'd been blessed with the ability to never meet a stranger.

"Maybe. But if you start over every couple of years, it seems like that would prevent you from ever being really close to anyone."

He'd only been around her three times, and she'd already

nailed him. For some reason her words stung. "I'm close enough. These days with e-mail and texting and Skype, it's easy to stay connected." He held up a heaping fork of pulled pork. "This is some good barbecue. Good call on the restaurant."

She raised an eyebrow but didn't say anything about his subject change. "It's one of my favorites. I'm something of a barbecue connoisseur."

He laughed. "Oh really? How exactly did you get that distinction?"

"My grandpa made the best barbecue in three counties. He even bottled his own sauce and sold it in a few shops back home for a little while. He always said I was his best helper. We'd sit out by the smoker, and he'd tell me stories about his childhood." She smiled at the memory.

Nick enjoyed watching her face light up as she talked about her family. "So where did this barbecue-making grandpa live? I take it you're not originally from here?"

She shook her head. "I'm a Mississippi girl. Born and raised along the delta in a town so small it's barely a speck on the map." She grinned. "It's not even on some maps."

"So when did you move to the city?"

She took another sip of tea. "I went to college at the University of Memphis and just stayed. After getting a taste of city life I couldn't imagine moving back to the boondocks. This was the biggest city I'd ever seen when I was a little girl, and I always had a soft spot for it."

"I had some friends who went to the U of M. I'll bet if we tried we could find acquaintances in common." Many of his classmates had attended Ivy League schools, but there were a few who'd attended one of the colleges in their hometown.

"How about you? Where'd you go to college?" she asked.

"Vanderbilt. And I loved it. Especially Nashville. In fact, I stayed there for a couple of years after graduation."

"I enjoy visiting Nashville. I have some friends there and go see them whenever I get the chance."

Nick's grandmother had been brokenhearted when he'd first moved away from Tennessee. She always said that as long as he lived within driving distance, she felt close to him. But he'd felt stifled in Nashville after a few years and had moved on. "So tell me about working at Graceland. Is that your dream job?" He always found it fascinating to hear people talk about finding their dream jobs. He liked what he did, but wasn't sure if it was a forever career.

She cocked her head. "Honestly? I never meant to work there but sort of fell into it. I started out as a teacher, believe it or not."

"Really? What grade?" He totally could see her as a teacher.

"Elementary. Third." She sighed. "I hated it. Except for the summers." She chuckled. "The kids were great; it was the other side of it that drove me crazy. Some of their recesses got cut out, and things just seemed so strict. All the mandates coming down from above seemed to suck the joy out of both teaching and learning. I wish I'd been one of those people who loved teaching enough to put up with all of that, but I wasn't. After a couple of years, I finally quit and started job hunting. That was about the time when the job market was really tight, so I pretty much applied for everything. I found an assistant event planning job at Graceland and thought it would be good until I found something I liked better." She shrugged. "But that hasn't happened. I got a promotion last year and haven't really made much effort to find anything else."

"You probably meet a lot of interesting people though, right?"

"Oh yeah. Don't get me wrong; I enjoy what I do. The thing that makes it worthwhile is that the visitors are so happy. Some of them have waited their whole lives to make the trek to see where Elvis lived. Others make it a yearly thing and meet up with other fans they've met through the years. It's like a big, international family reunion."

He chuckled. "I guess I never thought of it like that."

"And the weddings are awesome. The couples get a really unique experience. The fact that they choose to come to Graceland for their wedding means that they feel a special connection to the place. Lots of musicians choose to get married there. I don't mean the big names. I mean the guys who learned to play guitar at the knee of their grandpas or uncles and started out playing Elvis songs. It's incredibly rewarding to see those types marry at Graceland. They have Elvis music playing during the ceremony and have their pictures taken in front of the mansion." She grinned. "It's a unique job, that's for sure."

He nodded. "I'll say. But you said it wasn't your dream job. . . . What is?"

"Eventually I'd like to work with a nonprofit and do something that I'm really passionate about. Probably helping disadvantaged kids. I think we're all called to help people in some way. Some people do that through community outreach or volunteering. But I'd like to take it a step further and have it be my actual livelihood." She gave him a half smile. "I guess I just want to do something that matters in some way."

"That's noble."

She frowned. "I'm not trying to be noble."

"Oh, I didn't mean anything by that. I just meant that you have a good attitude toward work."

"Why? Because I see it as more than a paycheck?"

He nodded. "So many people can't see past the dollar signs."

"No one works at a nonprofit for the money." She laughed. "But no one teaches for it either. I guess I'm just destined to always be on the poor side. And that's fine. There's more to life than money."

He liked her perspective. He'd met so many people who made career decisions solely on the pay, and in his experience, those people were never satisfied. Not with the things they bought with their paychecks or with their lives in general. But he also knew this wasn't the time to mention his trust fund to her. She didn't seem like the kind of woman who'd be impressed by that anyway. Which was actually refreshing. "Sorry for all the questions. I hope you don't feel like I've been interviewing you."

Suzanne laughed. "That's fine. I'm not usually quite so forthcoming though. Did you secretly slip some truth serum into my tea?"

"You caught me. How else do you think I get the dirt for my freelance stories?" He chuckled. "Actually, you'd be amazed what people will share over a cup of coffee. Maybe we should try that sometime, and then you'd really tell me all of your secrets."

She laughed. "I don't know about that. A girl needs to keep some things to herself." She glanced at her watch. "Oh no! I've stayed too long. I've got to get back to work. We're getting ready for the official kickoff tonight. The midnight breakfast." She raised her eyebrows at him. "Sounds fun, huh? I might be able to get you an extra ticket, but you'd have to don a white jumpsuit and sideburns." She grinned, obviously kidding.

"Yeah, as tempting as that sounds, I think I'll pass." He chuckled. "Maybe next year."

"Whatever. Sounds like next year you'll be in Timbuktu or some such place."

He nodded. "True." He didn't want her to go yet. "This was fun. Would you like to have dinner again? I'd love the company. Maybe Friday?" Nick couldn't remember the last time he'd had two dinners in one week with the same woman. But he'd only be here for a short time, and she knew that. There wouldn't be any harm in seeing her again.

"Friday is tricky. There's an Elvis Week event at the Orpheum. It's the finals of the Ultimate Elvis Tribute Contest." She smiled. "But if you wouldn't mind dinner downtown, I'm in."

"Sounds great." He held up his cell phone. "I'll call you closer to Friday and confirm time and place." He furrowed his brow. "Guess we'll meet there again?"

She shrugged. "Unless you want to come with me to the Orpheum, in which case you can just come and pick me up."

Nick couldn't hide his smile. "That actually sounds fun. My grandmother will be so excited to hear it. She's a huge Elvis fan." He laughed. "She says she dated him when she was young, but I'm not sure about that."

Suzanne's laughter joined his. "I can't begin to tell you how many women come through who have that story." She shrugged. "Guess you never know." She stood and grabbed her purse from the back of her chair.

He started to rise, but she held out a hand to stop him.

"You stay. Finish your barbecue. No reason to walk me out." She grinned. "Talk to you later."

He watched her walk away wondering if Friday night would be a mistake. He enjoyed her company a lot more than he'd expected to.

And she certainly didn't fit into his future plans.

six

Suzanne's phone buzzed against her desk and she jumped. She'd been so engrossed in an e-mail detailing an upcoming wedding she'd tuned out everything around her. She grabbed the phone and answered.

"Miss Simpson?" a male voice on the other end of the line asked.

Suzanne held the phone back and glanced at the caller ID again. It was a local number, but she didn't recognize it. "This is Suzanne."

"This is Gary Anderson, with the property management company that takes care of your rental house. I was just calling to talk to you about your lease."

Suzanne wrinkled her forehead. Her lease wasn't up for another two months. She planned to stay put for at least another year. "Oh, yes. I'd like to go ahead and renew for another year."

Gary cleared his throat. "Actually, that's not going to be possible. The owner of the home has decided to sell. I was calling to give you a heads up in case you were interested in purchasing it. You have plenty of time to get the mortgage in place. But if not, we'll need to terminate the lease at the end of October."

Suzanne blew out a breath. This wasn't something she was prepared to deal with right now. *Why doesn't my life ever go like I plan?* She'd expected to live in her current home for another year and see if she found a new job by then. If so, then she'd thought she might find a new rental close by. "Thanks for letting me know. I don't think I'm interested in purchasing. Do you have any other rentals nearby though?" She loved her neighborhood in East Memphis. Starbucks and Target were close by. Her favorite takeout places were right around the corner. The park where she took Charlie to run was just down the street. The thought of leaving it made her sad. But not sad enough to commit to buying.

"We might have a couple more homes coming up for rent in the next couple of months. As you know, Colonial Acres is a popular area because of the easy proximity to everything, so we don't have rentals available there very often. I'll let you know though."

"Remember I need a place that will let me have a dog and that comes with a fenced-in yard." Suzanne didn't care about the number of bedrooms or bathrooms, or even the age of the home, as long as she was allowed to have Charlie. She'd never understood people who got rid of their dog because they moved into a place where dogs weren't allowed. She'd never consider moving to a place if Charlie couldn't come with her.

"I know one of the homes I'm thinking of has a no pet policy. I'll have to check on the other one," Mr. Anderson said.

"Okay. Thanks again for giving me plenty of notice." She ended the call and tossed her phone onto her desk. She buried her head in her hands.

"Problem?" Avis Thomas asked. Avis and Suzanne had started working at Graceland the same week and were what Suzanne always thought of as a classic example of "work friends." They shared details about their lives, but only up to a point. They might grab lunch but didn't see each other outside of work. Through the years, Suzanne had acquired a number of "work friends" and had the Christmas card list to prove it. But her closest friends, the ones who knew her well, were few in number.

"That was my landlord. My house is going up for sale when my lease is up. Which means I've got to find a new place to live." Suzanne sighed. "I hate moving. And packing. And looking at rental houses. Ugh."

Avis chuckled. "Girl, I don't know why you don't just break down and buy. You like your place, don't you?"

Suzanne nodded. "Yeah, but I'm not ready to buy."

"I'll bet your rent is twice what I pay on my mortgage." Avis shook her head. "Sometimes you've got to look at the bigger picture. You like your neighborhood. You're pouring money down the drain in rent. Not to mention that you'd be building equity."

Suzanne made a face. "I just don't think I want to buy yet. I'm not exactly sure where I want to live. I should probably try out another neighborhood before I do something so drastic."

Avis let out a peal of laughter. "Remind me again. How long have you lived in Memphis?"

"Eleven years."

"How many places have you lived in?"

Suzanne wrinkled her forehead. "Five. Not counting the semester in the dorm."

Avis sighed. "So six places in eleven years. And you don't have any intention of leaving Memphis, do you?"

Not now, but I like knowing I can pick up and leave whenever I feel like it. "Not anytime soon."

"Then maybe you should at least consider it. I promise you, the day I bought my first house was one of the proudest of my life. Second only to being the first in my family to graduate college." Avis beamed.

"I'm sure it would be a landmark kind of day. It's just one that I'm not sure I'm ready for."

"Maybe it's kind of like having kids. If you wait until you're ready, you'll never go through with it."

"Maybe." Was Avis right? And Emily? They'd both been encouraging her to consider home ownership. But something about it seemed so final. So settled. Suzanne enjoyed living her life knowing that if it weren't for Charlie, she could just put her things in storage and bum around Europe for a while. The thought comforted her in some strange way. Because sometimes she looked around at her friends who, the closer they got to thirty, were all starting to couple off and settle down. And quite frankly the thought of saying yes—whether it be to a man or to a home—terrified Suzanne.

Right to her very core.

❧

Nick couldn't stand to be in his grandmother's house. Maybe he should check into a hotel. The Peabody was sounding better and better. He armed the alarm and headed out to the car. Way too many family pictures adorned Grandmother's walls, and Nick couldn't help but stare at his parents' faces and wonder if they'd be disappointed in the way he'd turned out.

He drove aimlessly around Germantown until he ended up on Old Mill Drive. He pulled the car in front of the two-story brick home and killed the engine. The oak tree in front looked bigger than he remembered. But his mom's rosebushes at the side of the house looked exactly the same. He and Austin used to help her tend to the flowers. They'd water and pull weeds, and she'd laugh and tell them that when they were teenagers they should start their own lawn care business to make extra spending money. And they had, except that it only lasted one summer. Because by the time the next summer rolled around, Nick's parents and brother were gone.

A tap on the window made him jump. He glanced up to see an older man peering at him. Nick rolled down the window.

"You having car trouble, son?" the man asked.

Nick shook his head. "No sir, I used to live there when I was younger. I guess I just wanted to see the place."

The man smiled. "You must be the Taggart boy then? Madelyn Taggart's grandson?"

"Yes, sir. That's me." His grandmother knew everyone in Germantown.

"She comes over sometimes when the roses are in bloom and cuts a few to take home. Been doing that ever since I bought the place." He grinned. "I'm Thomas St. Claire."

The name sounded familiar to Nick. If he remembered correctly, Mr. St. Claire had been an executive for FedEx, but must be retired by now. His grandmother had been pretty picky about who bought the home, but the St. Claires had been friends of hers. "Nice to meet you."

"How is Madelyn doing? I know she's been having some health problems." The elderly man chuckled. "Of course, that's to be expected once you reach our age."

Nick quickly explained that his grandmother was in the hospital but was expected to be fine after a routine heart surgery.

Mr. St. Claire's weathered face grew somber. "Please give her my best. Madelyn has been a good friend to me since my wife passed away a couple of years ago."

"I will."

The older man gestured at Nick's childhood home. "Do you want to come in and see the place?"

Nick bit his bottom lip. Just seeing the outside of the home flooded him with memories of two little boys chasing each other around and playing hide-and-seek. If he went inside, he couldn't imagine how he would deal with the pain. "No thanks. Like I said, I was just driving by and thought I'd stop for a minute."

Mr. St. Claire smiled knowingly. "You've dealt with a tremendous loss, son. If you ever change your mind and want to stop in, you're welcome to."

"Thanks." Nick watched the elderly man amble toward the house. He shot Nick a wave before he went inside.

Nick sighed. He'd worked so hard to get away from this place, yet Memphis had always let out a siren call to him. And now that he was here, maybe it was time he faced his past and figured out how to move forward. But to what future? Nick had a great life drifting from place to place. But being here and seeing his roots made him long for something more.

He started the engine and headed out of the neighborhood that had been his home for seventeen years. His phone buzzed, and an unfamiliar Memphis number flashed on the screen. Could be the hospital. He clicked the SPEAKER button. "Hello?"

"Nick Taggart. I don't believe it." The male voice on the other end sounded familiar, but Nick couldn't place it.

"Who's speaking?"

The man burst out laughing. "Do you remember that night at the drive-in on Summer Avenue when we changed the movie and showed a video of Jennifer Lampton tripping during her sister's wedding?"

Nick chuckled. "Ryan Henderson. How in the world are you? And yes, I remember. It took Jennifer two years to forgive us, and even now I halfway expect her to pop up and retaliate because of what she considered the ultimate public humiliation." He'd had such a crush on Jennifer their sophomore year in high school. She'd attended Hutchison, the all-girls school whose campus had bordered his own school's campus. In hindsight, pulling such a prank had probably not been the way to win her heart. But it had been pretty funny to see her face as the scene unfolded on the big screen. He and Ryan had been banned from the drive-in for the rest of their high school career.

"I'm doing well. I thought I'd heard that you were going to be in town and wanted to see if we could get together sometime."

"That'd be great." Ryan had been his best friend from the time they were toddlers. Their losing touch had been Nick's fault. He'd even bowed out of being best man in Ryan's wedding after college graduation because he didn't want to come back to Memphis. He'd used work as an excuse but spent most of the next month bumming around Central America feeling like a jerk.

"How about Friday? Huey's?" The popular burger joint was a Memphis institution.

"I already have plans Friday. How about Saturday?"

Ryan groaned. "No can do. My youngest is turning three, and we're having ten pre-schoolers and a bunch of family members over." He laughed. "Lila would kill me if I went out after the party and left her to clean up and deal with two kids on sugar overload."

Nick couldn't fathom his old buddy as a dad. It didn't seem like they were old enough for those kinds of responsibilities, but each day brought him closer to thirty. He remembered a time when that had seemed so old. "I wouldn't want to get you in trouble with the wife. How about Sunday?"

"Sunday night after church would work. We usually get out around six, but you probably remember that." Ryan and Nick had grown up going to the same east Memphis church.

"How about we meet at six thirty? At the Huey's on Poplar?"

"See you then."

Nick turned the phone off and tossed it in the console. It would be nice to see Ryan again after all these years. They'd certainly had some fun times.

He merged the car onto the interstate and headed toward the hospital. Grandmother would be pleased that he had plans to see Ryan. And he suspected she'd be equally pleased that he'd stopped by and talked to Mr. St. Claire. She'd been after him to go by the old place ever since he got to town.

He'd leave out his upcoming date with Suzanne though. No reason to give Grandmother hope that he might decide to stay in Memphis for good.

Because no matter how nice the idea might sound to his grandma, that move wasn't in the cards for him.

seven

"I did something crazy today," Suzanne said into the phone. She'd just gotten into her car after a long day at work and was driving home to get ready for her date with Nick. Or whatever it was. Her outing with Nick? She wasn't clear if he considered it a date or not.

"What in the world did you do?" Emily asked. "Because let's face it, you're not exactly known for doing crazy things."

Suzanne laughed. "Okay. Crazy by my standards, boring to anyone else." She slowed down for a red light. "I signed up to run in the Elvis Presley 5K tomorrow. I know we aren't really at that point in our training yet, but it always looks like so much fun." The 5K had been held for more than twenty-five years, always during Elvis Week. The race started and ended at the gates of Graceland, and thousands of people ran or walked it, many decked out in their best Elvis attire. The proceeds always supported a great cause, and Suzanne had considered signing up for the past few years. And today in a weak moment, she'd registered.

"I wish I could do it with you, but I have to work late tonight. There's no way I'll be able to get up early for a run. But it's not that crazy. I think you'll do great."

She knew she could count on Emily for a pep talk. It was one reason she'd called. "Are you sure? What if I can't finish?"

"Don't be silly. No one says you have to run the entire time. Jog some and walk some, just like we do at the park. You'll do great. Besides, aren't there usually more than a thousand people running?"

"I think so."

"Then there's no way you'll be last." Emily giggled. "Surely in that big of a group there'll be someone slower than you."

Suzanne couldn't hold back her laughter. "Thanks a lot. Some cheerleader you are."

"I'm totally kidding, and you know it. We've been running for a few weeks now. I definitely think you can do it. Besides, this will be great practice for the St. Jude race. If you have trouble with this distance, maybe we really should switch from the half marathon to the 5K."

"Good idea. I'll let you know. If I have to be carried over the finish line, I'm definitely switching."

"Whatever." Emily sighed. "Is tonight the night you're going out with Airplane Guy?"

Suzanne laughed. "Nick. I told you his name is Nick."

"So we aren't just referring to this one by a nickname? He must be special." Emily always accused Suzanne of referring to her dates by nicknames to keep herself from getting too attached.

"Not special. Just that the nickname doesn't seem to fit him." She pulled into her driveway and turned the engine off.

Charlie barked a greeting from inside the house, and his face popped up in the window next to where her car was parked.

"Whatever you say. But have fun tonight. And good luck tomorrow. You'll have to fill me in on how it goes."

"You want to come to church with me on Sunday? We could have lunch afterward. I think Jade is back in town." Jade Denton had been the first person Suzanne met when she started attending a new church in Midtown. They'd become fast friends, and sometimes the three of them got together for a girls' night out.

"I really can't. I'm on call and will probably be at the hospital most of the day." No matter how many times Suzanne invited Emily to church, she always found an excuse why she couldn't come. But Suzanne would keep trying.

"Okay. Maybe some other time then. I'll talk to you soon." She tucked her phone into her purse and hurried inside. She and Emily had a lot in common, but Emily refused to discuss her faith—or lack of it. In all the years they'd been friends, Suzanne had only seen Emily inside a church for weddings or funerals. Suzanne's faith had gotten her through a lot of tough times. She couldn't imagine not having that. But Emily was stubborn and wouldn't even discuss it. *Lord, please open her heart, and show me how to be a light for You.*

"Hey, sweet boy," she said as she opened the door.

Charlie bounded out, stopping just long enough for her to pat him on the head before he set out to explore the backyard.

Suzanne hurried to get ready. She'd spoken to Nick on the phone last night, and they'd decided he'd pick her up. At first she'd hesitated. So much so that she'd almost called him and told him she'd have to meet him downtown. She didn't usually date guys from Memphis for a reason. Dating someone local would mean they would spend time at her house. In her space. That was too close for comfort for her.

But it was too late now. She glanced at the ornate clock that hung over her plush, red couch. He was probably already on his way.

She'd picked out her outfit last night, so at least she wouldn't have to stress over what to wear. She slipped on a dark red wrap dress. It had been one of her most recent purchases at Ann Taylor. She didn't splurge on clothes too often, but this dress looked like it was made for her. Emily had been with her and had threatened to buy it and give it to her for her birthday if she didn't get it for herself.

She slipped on her favorite pair of black strappy sandals and her diamond drop necklace to complete the look. She stood back and glanced in the full-length mirror at the end of the hallway. *Perfect.* A quick touch-up of her makeup and a spritz of hairspray and she was ready.

She filled Charlie's bowl with his favorite food and put it on the kitchen rug next to his water bowl. "Charlie," she called, holding the back door open. "Time to eat."

He ran inside and skidded to a stop at the sight of his full food bowl.

Suzanne chuckled and patted him on the head. She couldn't imagine life without Charlie. She'd gotten him when she first moved into an apartment during her freshman year of college. That had been ten years ago. She often joked that Charlie was her longest-standing, most successful relationship. *There's a grain of truth to every joke.*

At six o'clock on the dot, the doorbell rang. *Bonus points for promptness.* She waited a moment then walked to the front door. The butterflies in her stomach surprised her. Meeting for barbecue had been one thing. But his coming to pick her up for dinner downtown and an event at the Orpheum seemed much more intimate. She slowly opened the door, uncertainty creeping over her. What was she doing?

Nick stood on the porch, in khakis, a blue button-down, and a blue-and-green striped tie. He clutched a bouquet of pink gerbera daisies in one hand and a giant dog bone in the other.

Suzanne couldn't hide her smile. Even though he'd made it clear he was only in town for a short time, he'd brought his A game.

But that would mean she'd have to stay on guard against his charm and good looks. She hadn't given anyone access to her heart in a very long time.

No way was she going to lose it to a world traveler like Nick Taggart.

No way.

❧

Nick had worried that the flowers and dog bone were too much, but the broad smile on Suzanne's face made his gesture well worth it. He returned her grin. "For you." He handed her the flowers. "I had a feeling generic roses wouldn't do the trick."

She laughed. "Roses are nice, but you guessed correctly." She held up the bouquet. "These are much better." She gestured at the bone in his hand. "And I guess that's for Charlie?"

Nick nodded. "I figured I'd better try and get off on the right foot with him."

Suzanne raised her eyebrows. "Sneaky, trying to get Charlie on your side. I guess you know if he doesn't like you I'll have to toss you out."

Nick chuckled. "I figured. I was taking a gamble that old Charlie still likes bones."

She clapped her hands. "Charlie," she called loudly. "He's a little hard of hearing," she explained.

A boxer mix trotted into the living room. At the sight of Nick he stopped and let out a low growl. He maneuvered his way in between Nick and Suzanne, clearly going into protective mode.

"Easy boy," Nick said. He held out the bone toward Charlie. "You want this?"

Charlie glanced at Suzanne and then back to Nick. He slowly walked over and sat down in front of Nick.

"Here you go," Nick said.

The dog took the bone from him and carried it over to a plaid dog bed in the corner.

"Success," Nick said with a laugh. "The dog has given me clearance."

Suzanne grabbed her purse from the coffee table. "Congratulations. Looks like Charlie gives his approval. So I guess we can go."

Nick held the door open for her, and they stepped outside into the August heat. Memphis might not be in the deep South, but the heat and humidity could rival just about anywhere. The August heat reminded Nick of two-a-day football practices and the way he and the guys used to run through the sprinklers on their way back to the locker room. He quickly pushed the memory away. He didn't like to think about football anymore.

Suzanne locked the door and followed him to his grandmother's car.

He opened the passenger door for her, and she climbed inside. He couldn't help but notice her long, shapely legs. She'd mentioned the other night that she was a runner. It certainly paid off. He closed the door behind her. "You look beautiful, by the way," he said once they were on the way.

She grinned at him. "Thank you. You look nice, too."

"Would you believe that I didn't have a tie to wear? Whenever I move, I donate most of my stuff to Goodwill. Makes moving easy, but it means I had to do a little shopping today." He laughed as he turned the car north onto Mt. Moriah Road. "If I'm going to be here for a few weeks, maybe I'd better build up my wardrobe a little bit."

She laughed. "Well I'm honored that you chose to shop for tonight. I know the crowd at the Orpheum will probably be pretty casual tonight considering most of them have been out at Graceland today, but it's such a nice building I hated the thought of not dressing up."

As a boy, Nick loved watching his parents get ready to go out to the Orpheum. They'd dress to the nines. In the winter, his mom would wear a fur wrap, and she let him run his fingers over it. He and Austin would sit on the stairs and watch them leave. Nick had thought his mother was the most beautiful woman in the world and had idolized his dad. Once just before the accident, Dad had been out of town on work and Mom had tickets to see *Les Miserables*. Nick had gone with her, and she'd had him put on a coat and tie. *"The Orpheum is one of the grand theaters of the South. We should dress appropriately."* A week later, she was dead, and Nick had worn the same coat and tie to the funeral.

"You're not going on 240?" Suzanne's voice pulled him out of his memories.

He shook his head. "I thought we'd take Poplar all the way downtown and avoid the interstate. On the way over, I heard about a couple of wrecks on 240, and it sounds like traffic is pretty backed up."

"Typical Friday afternoon in Memphis," she said. "Poplar is

fine. I go that way a lot when I have to go downtown. A lot of stoplights, but it's better than sitting still on the interstate."

Nick brought the car to a stop as they waited for the light to change. "I made dinner reservations." He glanced at her. "I hope that's okay."

Suzanne's eyes sparkled. "Reservations? You're really trying to get bonus points tonight, aren't you? On time, flowers, bone for Charlie, and now this?" She ticked them off on her hand.

"Is it working? Because I figure I need all the bonus points I can use."

She giggled. "So far, so good. I haven't bailed yet, have I?" She smiled. "Where did you make reservations?"

"The Majestic Grille." He maneuvered into the far lane. Poplar was bumper to bumper. Must be a lot of people headed downtown tonight.

"That's one of my very favorites. I go to shows at the Orpheum sometimes with two of my best friends, and we always try and eat there."

"Whew." He mocked wiping sweat from his brow. "Glad to know you approve of the choice. It came highly recommended by one of the nurses at the hospital." He'd struck up a conversation with his grandmother's nurse and asked her for suggestions of places he should eat while he was in town. He'd been careful not to mention that he was taking a date, otherwise his grandmother would've grilled him.

"How is she?" Suzanne asked quietly.

He shrugged. "Her blood pressure is high. They're trying to get it down before they do the surgery. But I talked to the doctor this morning, and he expects her to come through just fine. She's in good hands." One thing he had to admit, Memphis had some of the best medical facilities in the country. He'd been impressed a couple of years ago when he'd read about one of the wealthiest men in the world choosing to have a life-saving transplant in Memphis. It was a testament to the city.

"That's great. I'm sure everything will go fine. I'll keep her in my prayers."

He glanced over at her from the corner of his eye. "Thanks." He'd traveled all over the world and had dated women from all walks of life. But none of them had been as beautiful or as desirable to him as Suzanne was at this moment, offering prayers for his grandmother. "So tell me more about you. What's a typical weekend like? I mean, when you're not going to see fake Elvises perform."

"What do you mean? That's a weekly occurrence for me." She chuckled. "Kidding. A typical weekend. . ." She trailed off for a long moment. "Well a lot of times on Friday night after work, I meet up with my friend Jade for dinner or a movie. Saturdays if I don't have a work event, I take Charlie for a run and maybe do a little shopping. Sometimes I go out on Saturday night. And then Sunday is church and, if I'm lucky, a nap." She shrugged. "That's pretty much it. Boring, right?"

"Sounds perfect," Nick said with a grin. "But I want to know about that vague 'sometimes I go out on Saturday night' bit." He glanced at her and enjoyed the pink blush that crept up her cheeks.

"What do you mean?" she asked innocently.

He laughed. "I guess I'm just surprised that a girl like you hasn't already been snatched up. That's all."

"A girl like me? What exactly does *that* mean?" She furrowed her brow.

He pulled the car into the Peabody Place parking garage and rolled the window down to get a ticket from the automated dispenser. "Smart, pretty, and obviously of high moral character." He pulled into an empty space and looked over at her. "Seems to me that your companionship is probably in high demand, that's all."

She met his gaze and held it for a long moment. "My life is exactly the way I want it. Uncomplicated. Most of the guys I date are from out of town. I've only been in a serious relationship one time, and that was when I was in college. Since then, I choose not to. I'm telling you this because I sense that you're the same way. Otherwise you'd have put down some roots by now."

He nodded. "It's surprising though. I thought all women were chomping at the bit to settle down once they reached a certain age."

"What are you trying to say? That I'm old? And by the way, horses chomp at the bit, not women. I'm beginning to see why you're single."

"That came out all wrong." *Smooth, dude. Very smooth.* "I just meant that I've never met a woman who wasn't looking to settle down."

"Well now you have." She opened the car door. "Let's go. I'm starving."

He got out of the car and shut the door. Suzanne stood at the back of the car with her arms crossed. He'd never met anyone like her. "I didn't mean to offend you. Do you think I could get a do-over? And maybe you could forget that I accidentally compared women to horses?" He offered a tentative smile.

She laughed. "I'm not offended. You were just asking. And

believe me, I know I'm not like most women my age. With each passing day I realize how much of a weirdo I am. I mean, my friends can't wait to settle down and have families. And I can't even think about buying a house without practically breaking out in hives." She sighed. "It's not that I never want to get married and have a family. It's just that I second-guess myself a lot. It's easier to stay away from decisions that have the ability to alter my life in a big way. I figure that at some point down the road, I'll be over it." She grinned. "But until then, it's off the table."

"Which is why most of the guys you date are from out of town, right? Because it's hard to have serious expectations in a long-distance relationship." He got it. It actually sounded a lot like something he would do. Something he had done.

"Exactly." She widened her eyes.

"And then, let me guess? When they do start expecting things, that's when you drop the 'I'm not interested in a long-distance relationship' bomb, right?"

She laughed. "It's like you're in my head. Yes, that's pretty much how it goes down. In fact, I'd been dropping one such bomb when we met. That's why I was passing through Atlanta."

Nick shook his head. Was it possible he'd finally met his match? But knowing where she stood made it much easier to relax. He'd been hesitant coming into this night because he'd been a little too eager to see her again.

But Suzanne was clearly not looking for a real relationship either. So that meant he could just enjoy spending time with her.

No strings attached.

eight

Once they'd placed their orders, Suzanne peered across the table at Nick. "So isn't there anything you miss about Memphis? You act like it's a real burden to be here." She still hadn't quite figured out why he seemed to have such a chip on his shoulder about the city.

"Sometimes I miss the familiar sights. The way the river rolls past Tom Lee Park. The Pyramid hovering over downtown. The line of people outside of Gus's Chicken, just waiting for a table." He grinned. "I always tell people that Memphis is really a small town masquerading as a metropolis. I miss the way I always used to run into people I knew, no matter where I went."

She nodded. "True."

The waitress carefully placed two glasses of tea and an order of spinach and artichoke dip in front of them. "Your food will be out soon," she said. "Let me know if y'all need anything else."

"Mind if I pray?"

She shook her head. "You don't have to ask me that anymore. I'll never mind. In fact, I'll always be glad for you to pray."

Nick smiled. "Good to know." He quickly thanked God for the food and asked Him to be with them throughout the evening and the rest of their days. "So am I to assume that you're a religious person?" he asked when the prayer was over.

Suzanne nodded. "Yes. I guess I'm probably like a lot of people in that when I was younger I think I just followed along with my family and their beliefs. But as I've gotten older, I've developed my own faith and my own beliefs. I'm blessed to have made some great friends at church who really strengthen and encourage me. How about you?"

He nodded. "Much the same. I was brought up attending church regularly and was active in the youth group and all that. But it wasn't until I was out on my own that I really formed my own relationship with Jesus. And now that I travel all over the place, I feel like I've really learned more about what it means to worship. Sometimes I feel much closer to Him out in nature than I ever do sitting in a pew." He shrugged. "I guess you never really stop growing spiritually. At least that seems to be the lesson I've learned over the past years."

People didn't surprise Suzanne very often, but Nick continued to do so. She remembered the snap judgment she'd made when she first saw him on the plane. She'd noticed the way he wore his baseball cap low over his eyes and jumped to the conclusion that he was a partying frat boy like so many of the guys she'd known in college. But that seemed to be miles away from the truth. "I agree." She grinned. "You know, you're pretty insightful."

Nick twisted his mouth into a smile. "Do I detect some surprise there?"

She laughed. "Maybe a little. I'm guilty of expecting the worst from people." She'd been disappointed so many times, she found it easier to automatically expect the worst-case scenario.

The waitress placed two heaping plates in front of them.

"Looks delicious," Nick said, cutting into his steak.

Suzanne leaned over her pasta dish, basking in the scent. "Smells good, too." She took a bite. "So tell me this, Mr. World Traveler. Do you not get lonely traipsing all over the place? Surely you at least have a dog or something to keep you company."

Nick shook his head. "Are you kidding? I don't even have a fish. I'm not around enough to take care of a pet. They're just too much responsibility." He spooned some sour cream onto his baked potato. "But I love dogs though. I had one when I was a kid and loved him. Maybe someday I'll be in a position to have another pet. In the meantime, I can always volunteer at an animal shelter whenever I need my dog fix." He grinned.

She didn't want to point out how sad and lonely that life sounded. Even though she'd always said she liked the idea of being able to put her things in storage and bum around Europe, it seemed like it would be a lonely existence. "I guess. I can't imagine life without Charlie though." She shook her head. "Sunday night when I got home from Atlanta, it was too late to pick him up from the boarder. My house felt totally empty."

Nick shrugged. "Guess if I was used to coming home to a pet every night I'd feel that way. But I'm not, so my empty place just seems very peaceful to me." He gave a little smile. "Besides, I don't stay home much anyway."

She identified with him to a point. But she couldn't help but wonder what made him so scared of letting people into his life. She might not be ready to settle down, but she had close relationships. From what she could tell of Nick, he kept everyone at an arm's length. "We should probably get going soon." She smiled. "I know you'd hate to miss the opening."

He chuckled. "You're right about that." He flagged down the waitress and pulled out his wallet.

Suzanne reached for her purse. She might've let him pay for the barbecue the other night, but dinner at the Majestic Grille was in a different league.

"Put your purse away. This is my treat." He winked. "And I won't even try and put the moves on you at the end of the night; I promise."

She laughed. "Thanks."

He placed some cash on the table and guided her out of the restaurant.

The feel of his hand on the small of her back sent delicious shivers up her spine. There was just something about him. . . . She would have to be very careful not to fall under his spell. She'd had her heart broken once a long time ago.

And it was not an experience she intended to repeat.

❧

Nick resisted the urge to take her hand as they walked the short distance to the Orpheum. He hadn't been this attracted to a woman in he didn't know how long. Maybe ever. And it was more than just her looks. She put him at ease. Just now, over dinner, he'd had the feeling that they'd known each other forever. "So what exactly happens tonight?" He shoved his hands in his pocket to keep from reaching for her. "I have to admit, growing up here I just assumed everything going on that had to do with Elvis was geared toward tourists. So I'm not even sure what goes on during Elvis Week."

"Tonight is the finals of the ultimate Elvis tribute contest," she explained. "The guys are from all over the world and have been competing all week. So this is the best of the best as far as impersonators go. There will probably be some depicting Elvis as he looked when he first started out and others who will be in the traditional white jumpsuit with rhinestones." She grinned. "So just think of tonight as a little walk down memory lane, Elvis-style."

He chuckled. "Wow." He held the door open for her at the Orpheum, and they followed the crowd inside.

She pulled two tickets out of her purse and handed them to the doorman.

He scanned the tickets and handed them back. "Enjoy the show."

Suzanne gestured at a huge, red-carpeted staircase. "We're up in the balcony." They climbed up the ornate staircase and headed toward their section.

His cell phone buzzed just as they got to the door that led to their seats. He pulled it from his pocket. It was Richard, his editor. "This is work. Do you mind if I take it? I'll only be a second."

She shook her head. "Take your time." She handed him a ticket. "I'll see you inside."

He hit the button and raised the phone to his ear. "Hey, Richard."

"What's going on down there, man? I haven't heard from you in a week."

"I'm still in Memphis. My grandmother's surgery has been postponed, so it looks like I'll be here awhile longer. But you're not going to believe where I am."

Richard groaned. "Do I even want to know? Probably some backwoods Tennessee place that would scare a city boy like me. Am I right?" he asked with a laugh.

"It's Elvis Week here," Nick explained. "Thousands of people descend upon Memphis to celebrate the life and career of Elvis. It's held every year around the anniversary of his death. It's serious business."

"So what, you're at Graceland or something?" Richard asked.

"Actually I'm downtown at the ultimate Elvis tribute contest." The lights in the hallway flashed. That usually meant five minutes until showtime. "So these guys will be like the best Elvis impersonators in the world."

Richard laughed. "That's too much, man. Hey, you think there's a story down there for Elvis Week? Like what makes people still care or how nuts do you have to be to attend? Something like that?"

"I was hoping you'd think so. I'll get on it." The lights flashed again. "I've got to run. They're about to start. I'll be in touch soon." He ended the call and set his phone to silent. Now to find Suzanne. He showed his ticket to the woman at the door, and she motioned for him to follow her. She guided him to the center of the building and pointed at one of the roped-off boxes. "Thanks," he said. He walked down two steps and settled into the seat next to Suzanne. "Nice seats."

She raised her eyebrows. "Job perk."

The house lights went down and the crowd cheered. If they were this excited about fake Elvises, Nick couldn't imagine what a real Elvis show had been like. Must have been crazy. He'd have to ask his grandmother.

Two hours later, he and Suzanne shuffled their way down the stairs. The crowd pressed in on both sides, and without thinking, he reached down and took her hand.

She glanced over at him, a startled expression in her eyes.

"Hope this is okay. I don't want you to get crushed or anything." He grinned, enjoying the feel of her hand in his. She had dainty hands. And he appreciated that she had painted fingernails. It was a little thing, but so feminine.

"It's fine." She squeezed his hand. "In fact, I kind of like it."

They followed the crowd out into the hot Memphis night. Despite the late hour, downtown was crowded. Nick tugged on her hand. "You mind if we stroll down Beale Street? I haven't been there in forever."

She smiled. "Fine by me. But I can't stay out late. I'm running in a 5K tomorrow morning."

They walked slowly past the parking garage where Nick had parked. "Let me guess. Is it an Elvis-themed 5K?" he asked.

Suzanne giggled. "Guilty."

Nick thought back to his conversation with Richard. Surely the Elvis 5K would be full of interesting tidbits he could use in an article. "How about we make it interesting?"

She stopped on the sidewalk and narrowed her eyes at him. "What do you mean?"

He grinned. "I'll run, too. Loser has to buy dinner one night next week."

Suzanne cocked her head. "Why do I get the feeling that I'm going to see a lot of you while you're in town?"

He pulled her closer to him. "Because you are," he said softly. He wanted to kiss her, but it wouldn't be right. That would only bring real feelings into their relationship, and that was the last thing either of them needed.

They walked hand in hand to Beale Street where the bright lights beckoned. "It's awfully crowded tonight," Suzanne remarked. "Don't these people know how late it is?" She giggled. "Clearly I'm not much of a 'stay out late' kind of girl."

The Beale Street crowd was a mix of college students, bachelorette parties, and music lovers. When Nick lived in Memphis, he'd been too young to get into many of the establishments on the famed street, but several restaurants offered live music and welcomed all ages. They walked past B.B. King's Blues Club, a restaurant and blues club. The facade of the place was often depicted in movies or TV shows set in Memphis. "I'm guessing most of these people will be here until all the places shut down. And I agree. I think my staying-out-all-night days are behind me." Nick chuckled at a kid turning flips for a small crowd and dropped a dollar in his tip bucket. For more than twenty years, kids had been turning flips on Beale Street to entertain the crowds and pick up some extra cash. A few years ago, a group of them even competed on a talent search TV show and showcased their acrobatics.

"Are you a big music fan?" Suzanne asked as a blues riff blared out of a dive bar they walked past.

Nick shrugged. "I don't play or anything, but I love live music. I grew up on the Beatles and the Rolling Stones. My parents always had music playing. Dad used to say that every life had a soundtrack." He'd forgotten that until just now. It was funny the things he'd forgotten over the years and the way those memories floated back at unexpected times.

"I like that," Suzanne said. "And it's so true. I have music playing almost all the time. At work, in my car, even when I run." She grinned. "My life's soundtrack is kind of eclectic."

Nick sighed with relief as she let the mention of his parents pass by without commenting. He wasn't trying to be deceitful with her, but he wasn't ready to share that much of himself with anyone. And he wasn't sure if he'd ever be. It had nothing to do with Suzanne and everything to do with his own fear of getting too close to someone. Because once he let someone in, they'd have the capacity to hurt him. And he didn't like that lack of control. Nick preferred the upper hand. "Eclectic, huh? So what's on your soundtrack?"

"A little country. Mostly old-school stuff though. George Strait. Alabama. Maybe some Taylor Swift thrown in to keep it current. And then a little Jimmy Buffett for days I feel like the beach." She grinned. "Huey Lewis is my favorite to sing along to in the car. And I think I own pretty much every U2 song ever recorded, so a lot of those would be on my soundtrack for sure." She tugged on his hand. "How about you?"

"A lot of the same." He was surprised at how in sync their taste was. "Except for the Taylor Swift." He shot her a smile. "And then I'd add the Beatles and a couple of big-haired 80s bands."

She laughed. "Right. I left off the big-haired bands."

Nick shrugged. "I've always had hair envy. Maybe that's why mine is a little longer than it probably should be." His grandmother had given him a hard time this morning about his shaggy hair. He figured as long as it barely grazed his collar, he was still okay. "Guess we should go. Especially if I'm going to get over there in the morning in time to register to run."

She glanced up at him. "So you're really coming in the morning?"

He nodded. "Yep. And remember. . .loser buys dinner."

"Sounds like a plan."

He enjoyed the feel of her hand in his as they strolled back to the parking garage. The ease in which they related to one another worried him.

But not enough to decide not to see her again.

nine

Suzanne pulled into the designated parking lot at Graceland. It was already boiling hot outside, and the prospect of running three miles didn't sound nearly as appealing today as it had yesterday when she'd signed up. But she hated to back out, especially since Nick was supposed to run with her.

Or at least he'd said he was going to show up. For all she knew he'd hit the snooze button just like she'd wanted to do.

She hid her purse and keys beneath the passenger seat. She'd tie her spare car key on her shoestring. She climbed out of the SUV and walked around to the back of the vehicle. She quickly pinned her race bib to her T-shirt and put the timing chip on her shoe.

Once she was finished stretching, she headed toward the starting line. No sign of Nick yet, but fifteen minutes remained until race time. Surely he'd show.

Suzanne put in her earbuds and selected the music app on her iPhone. She'd made a special playlist for the 5K. She did a few more stretches and glanced around at the growing crowd gathered at the starting line. She whirled as someone tapped her on the shoulder.

A grinning Nick stood before her, his race bib slightly crooked on his T-shirt.

Suzanne pulled one of the earbuds out of her ear. "Hey there. I wasn't sure if you'd show."

"Are you kidding? And miss the chance for you to buy me dinner?" Nick lunged forward to stretch his leg.

"You're certainly confident. I didn't realize you were a runner."

He smirked. "Well, I'm not a runner per se, but I spend a lot of time at the gym. I figure if I can handle the elliptical, I can handle a few miles."

"The gym is air conditioned"—Suzanne waved an arm around—"The great outdoors are not."

Nick laughed. "You're right about that. I admit, I'm a little worried about the heat. But I heard a lady at the registration table say that a lot of the homeowners in the neighborhood we'll be running through will have their sprinklers turned on and put out at the curb so we can cool off as we run."

"Gotta love that good ol' Southern hospitality, right?" She asked with a chuckle.

A man with a loudspeaker began to make announcements at the front.

Suzanne nudged Nick. "I'm going to run with my earbuds in, so don't expect me to talk to you."

He laughed and pointed at the iPod attached to an armband on his arm. "I doubt I could talk and run at the same time anyway, so I brought mine, too. In fact, I made a special playlist."

"Full of big-haired 80s bands, no doubt," Suzanne teased.

Nick nodded. "Yes, ma'am. Everything from Bon Jovi to Night Ranger with a little bit of Poison thrown in for good measure." He smiled and looked her up and down. "You look pretty cute as a sporty girl."

She adjusted her Memphis Tigers baseball cap. "My hair

is still too short for a ponytail. I figured this was the best way to keep it under control." She was in the process of deciding whether to keep her hair short or grow it out again, but there was no reason to let Nick in on her internal debate. Most days she liked the shorter style, but then days like this came, and she missed a ponytail something fierce.

"It's cute." He reached out and tapped the brim of her cap. "I always did like a girl who could rock a baseball cap." He jerked his chin toward the front of the line. "It looks like we're just about to start. See you at the finish line?"

She nodded. "You got it. May the best runner win."

He laughed. "And may the worst runner choose dinner wisely."

The guy with the loudspeaker counted them down and blew an air horn.

Suzanne stuck her earbuds back in her ears and turned up the volume. She fell in line behind an older lady in head-to-toe spandex and then jogged over the starting line. The instructions on the timing chip had said that each person's time would start once the chip crossed the line. Which meant she was officially on the clock.

She kept a slow and steady pace for the first three songs on her playlist but realized she was going to have to walk for a couple of minutes. She jogged over to the far side of the crowd and slowed to a walk. She'd lost sight of Nick almost immediately. He'd gone on and on about the loser buying dinner, which she was fine with. She wasn't really in a competition with him, but with herself. She knew it would do a lot for her confidence as a burgeoning runner if she could complete the 5K with a decent time.

Ever since she'd gotten up this morning, a verse from the fourth chapter of Second Timothy had been running through her head. *I have fought the good fight, I have finished the race, I have kept the faith.* There had been so many times in the past when she'd seen her faith falter. When good things happened, it was easy to have faith. But when the hard times came, that's when it was tougher.

Suzanne felt a sense of accomplishment once she passed the first mile marker. Her goal was in reach. *I have finished the race.* She couldn't wait to prove to herself once and for all that she could finish. And she couldn't help but think about the rest of her life as she ran toward her running goal. Was it time to seriously consider becoming a homeowner? Could she finally let go of the fear that held her back and finally trust that the Lord had a plan for her? And would she ever be able to trust anyone enough to make him a permanent part of her life?

Only time would tell.

❧

Nick slowed his pace after he grabbed water from the water station at the two-mile mark. He'd lost sight of Suzanne in the crowd, but every now and then he thought he saw her bright blue cap in the sea of people. This race was much harder than he'd anticipated.

He pulled his shirt away from his body and waved it back and forth to let in some air. He should've worn one of those moisture-wick shirts instead of just a regular T-shirt. Next time he'd know better. Next time. Maybe there wouldn't be a next time. He didn't stay in one place long enough to get to know the 5K calendar.

A group of guys dressed like Elvis, complete with sideburns, jogged past him. *That is definitely going in the article.* He shook his head as the morning sunshine glinted off their rhinestone jumpsuits.

He approached the three-mile mark, and the runners in his group kicked it into high gear. Only two-tenths of a mile left. Nick pumped his legs and broke into a full-speed run.

Suzanne appeared out of nowhere, her blue cap bobbing. She flashed him a smile as she drew up beside him.

No way was he going to let a girl beat him, even one who'd been training when he hadn't. He matched her stride step for step, and they crossed the finish line at the same time.

Nick ran through the queue for male runners, and once he was through, he stopped. He put his hands on his knees and tried to take a few deep breaths.

"Good form out there," Suzanne said, coming up next to him. She held out a cup of water she'd grabbed from the table at the finish line.

He took the water from her. "Thanks." He tossed back the cup and drained the water.

"There's quite a party set up in the plaza," she said.

He motioned toward the sidewalk. "Lead the way."

They headed toward the plaza. "I guess it was a tie, huh?" he asked.

Suzanne burst out laughing. "You really are competitive, aren't you?" She bumped him with her shoulder. "Actually, if you must know, I'm pretty sure you beat me by just a hair. But I think they'll post the official times soon."

Nick chuckled. "Yeah, being competitive is one of my bad habits." He'd grown up playing sports, and the drive to win had been present from an early age. Even though he'd stopped playing team sports when he was a junior in high school, he'd still competed in other avenues. In college it had been grades. Now that he was an adult, he wanted to be the best at whatever he did, whether it was writing an article for a magazine or investing in the stock market.

"Nothing wrong with a little competition as long as you keep it in check." Suzanne motioned toward a huge tent with tables set up. "Ooh, it looks like they have doughnuts for us. I think I could run a 5K every day if it meant I could eat those without any guilt."

Nick nodded. "Me, too." He motioned for her to enter the tent first and followed behind her in line. He filled his plate with a chicken biscuit and two doughnuts. He grabbed a bottle of Gatorade from an ice chest and followed Suzanne over to a sidewalk where a number of runners were sitting and eating. "Man, if I'd known 5Ks came with a spread like this, I'd have started running a long time ago."

Suzanne giggled. "No doubt."

Nick appreciated the way her makeup-free face glowed from the exertion of the run. Her eyes were nearly as blue as her cap, and her full, pink lips didn't need any lipstick to make them as enticing as any he'd ever seen.

Her mouth curved into a smile. "Are you checking me out?"

He laughed. "Maybe a little." He cast her a sideways glance. "Just mentally comparing the woman I was with last night to the one sitting next to me today."

"And? Which do you prefer?" she asked teasingly.

He shook his head. "Tough call. I mean, last night's date was all decked out in a dress and heels and all. But I have to admit there's something alluring about running shorts and no makeup." He threw his hands up in surrender. "It's a toss-up, I guess."

She laughed. "Well, to be honest, this is more me." She gestured at her exercise clothes. "But getting all fixed up is fun every now and then, too."

Nick watched as a guy in a Memphis Runners shirt tacked pages up on a board. "I think the results are in. . . . You ready?"

Suzanne stood and dusted off her shorts. "Are you kidding? I was *born* ready."

Laughing, they tossed their trash in one of the large cans nearby and made their way over to the results board.

"Here I am," Nick said, sliding his finger down the results for men in his age bracket. "Thirty-seven minutes and forty-four seconds. You?"

She groaned. "You're not going to believe this. Thirty-seven minutes and forty-*six* seconds."

"And by the smallest of margins, Nick Taggart wins the contest," he said in his best sports announcer voice. "A two-second victory, ladies and gentlemen. What will Miss Simpson fix for his victory dinner?"

Suzanne laughed. "How do you feel about letting the good people of Domino's Pizza take care of that?" She grinned.

"The lady knows the way to a man's heart is pizza," he said with a smile.

"How about Monday night? My place?" she asked.

A night at home with Suzanne sounded perfect. "Works for me. And I'll bring another bone for Charlie, just in case."

She laughed. "Sounds like a plan."

Nick walked her out to her car. He couldn't help but feel a little disappointed. He knew they'd just gone out last night, but he'd kind of hoped their dinner would be tonight. Maybe she already had another date though.

Even though he knew he had no claim on her and had no intention of having a claim on her, he hated the idea of her spending time with someone else. As he climbed into his grandmother's car, he was overcome with an unfamiliar feeling.

Jealousy.

ten

Suzanne wouldn't want to admit it to anyone, but her calf muscles were killing her. She'd hobbled through the parking lot at church and then forced herself to walk normally once she stepped inside the building. But after sitting still in the pew for more than an hour during the morning worship service, she was finding it hard not to hobble as she left the building.

"Um... Are you okay?" Jade Denton looked at her curiously. Her dark hair hung in waves around her face and made her green eyes stand out from her pale skin. "You have a weird expression on your face."

Suzanne clung to the pew in front of her. "I think my legs are going to fall off," she confessed through gritted teeth. "I ran in a 5K yesterday, and I guess I didn't stretch good enough or something."

Jade burst out laughing. "Those shoes probably aren't helping." She pointed at Suzanne's high heels.

Suzanne rolled her eyes. "I have one pair of flats that aren't flip-flops, and wouldn't you know it? Charlie decided to turn one of them into a chew toy last night. I guess I fell asleep on the couch and didn't wake up when he wanted to go outside. Because when I finally woke up, he'd chewed my shoe to pieces and had the most satisfied expression on his face." She couldn't help but smile.

"He knows how to push your buttons, doesn't he?" Jade

worked for the Memphis zoo and was always touting a study on the different personalities animals had. "He's figured you out over the years."

Suzanne nodded. "Well, he definitely won the argument."

"So are we on for lunch still?" Jade grinned. "Or do you need to go home and prop those feet up?"

Suzanne gingerly tested a few steps. "No. I'm starving and have zero groceries at home. And I certainly don't feel like walking through the supermarket today." She grinned. "What are you in the mood for?"

"How about Blue Plate?" The Blue Plate Café served breakfast and country cooking. It was one of their favorite after-church spots.

Suzanne nodded. "Perfect. Meet you there?"

"Yes. You want to invite Emily?" Jade and Emily had met through Suzanne but were friends now in their own right.

Suzanne shook her head. "Already did. She's on call and can't make it."

Twenty minutes later, they were seated and had ordered at the restaurant.

"So tell me what's been going on with you," Jade said. "I ran into Emily the other day, and she mentioned something about a guy and an airplane. . . . What's the deal?"

Suzanne filled Jade in on Nick. "This will sound crazy, I know. I've always thought that if a certain kind of guy came along, it might make me consider settling down. And Nick is that kind of guy." She laughed. "Of course, the only problem is that he has no interest in that either. He's definitely a footloose-and-fancy-free kind. Travels a lot and keeps everyone at an arm's length."

Jade wrinkled her forehead. "So you're going to let him just leave after his grandmother gets better? You don't plan to tell him that you're interested?"

Suzanne shook her head. "What's the point? I may be way off base anyway. For all I know a couple more dates and I'll see that we're totally incompatible. Which I'm sure is the case." Although the past couple of days had been fun. "At first I thought that since I knew he was only here temporarily, it would make it easy to just hang out and have a good time. But instead it makes it harder. I've been having such a good time with him that I've sort of put my guard up. The last thing I want to do is fall for someone who is about to leave."

"There's always long distance though, right?" Jade had never understood Suzanne's preference for long-distance relationships.

Suzanne shook her head. "Not this time. With Nick I'd either want everything or nothing at all. He and I are just. . ." She trailed off for a long moment. "We're alike. I don't know how to explain it exactly. But we seem to see eye to eye on a lot of things. I think we look at the world the same way." She lifted her glass as the waitress placed their food on the table.

"That's going to be hard to let go of even if you have your guard up, as you say," Jade observed. She sipped her sweet tea and gazed at Suzanne, her green eyes thoughtful. "But at least you've got someone to have a good time with for a little while. That's more than I have." She sighed.

Jade had always been the most serious of the three friends. Where Suzanne dated for fun and Emily dated because she attended a lot of social functions and hated to go alone, Jade had always looked for Mr. Right. She didn't accept dates with just anyone, so whenever she went out with someone new, Suzanne knew it meant something. "Dry spell?" Suzanne asked.

Jade nodded. "I went out a couple of times with a teacher. I thought he was a good prospect, but the last time we went out he was more concerned with his truck than he was with me."

Suzanne drew her brows together. "How so?"

Jade let out a small laugh. "This is one of those dating horror stories that only happen to me. We went to Starbucks after dinner, and the only parking space was next to this giant bush. When we went back later to get in the truck it was raining. Even so, he made me stand in the middle of the parking lot so he could back the truck up and get me. He was afraid that I might scratch his truck door on that stupid bush if I opened it where it was parked."

Suzanne burst out laughing. "Okay, that is bad. I'm guessing there won't be another date?"

Jade shook her head. "Nope." She grinned. "Your temporary relationship with Nick is sounding better and better, isn't it?"

"Compared to that, yes." She absently played with her straw wrapper. "I'm seeing him again tomorrow night." She couldn't keep the smile from her face. "I think that will be the one that will tell me if we're really compatible. We aren't doing anything. Just staying in and ordering pizza."

"Wow. When's the last time you did *that* on a date?"

Suzanne shook her head. "Years ago. Maybe when I was in college and was dating Chad." Ever since then, Suzanne had kept her home off-limits. Because when someone was comfortable enough to just hang out and have a quiet dinner and watch TV, it meant the relationship was shifting toward permanence. At least Suzanne had always thought that. So she'd only accepted dates that were activities: dinner, a movie, a concert. Never just hanging out at home. It looked like that would change tomorrow night.

❧

Nick hadn't had the heart to go to the church he grew up in. Instead, he'd driven out to a mega church near the Wolfchase Galleria mall. He figured with hundreds of people in attendance, he'd just be a face in the crowd.

Even though he had indeed blended in among the throng of people, there'd been a moment during the service when he'd wished he'd joined his childhood congregation. He visited their website sometimes and knew they still had the same preacher. In fact, no matter where in the world Nick was, if he had a bad day, he'd log on and listen to an archived sermon. Sometimes he could even pick out his grandmother's high soprano voice during the song services.

He drove straight to the hospital after church. He knew his grandmother was going stir-crazy. Yesterday, she'd told him that if her surgery didn't happen as scheduled this week, she was going to insist the doctor send her home. And one thing he knew about Madelyn Taggart, she usually managed to get her way.

He tapped on the door.

"Come in," she called.

Nick pushed the door open and was surprised to see Mr. St. Claire sitting at Grandmother's bedside. "I didn't know you'd have company," he said.

Grandmother beamed. "Thomas came by after church to bring me a bulletin. Wasn't that thoughtful?"

Nick fought to hide his smile. From the looks these two were giving one another, he'd guess that Mr. St. Claire must be something of a suitor. "That was very thoughtful. Nice to see you again, Mr. St. Claire." He shook the elderly man's outstretched hand.

"Please, call me Thomas." He grinned.

Grandmother piped up. "I hear you went to visit the old house. I'm so glad. The place looks nice, don't you think?"

Nick nodded. "The roses look the same."

Grandmother motioned toward a vase in the corner. "Thomas brought me a few pretty blooms today." She smiled broadly.

"Nick, what have you been doing to keep busy while you're in town?" Thomas asked.

Nick sat down in an empty chair. "I ran in a 5K yesterday, and Friday night I went to the Orpheum to see the Elvis tribute finals." He hadn't mentioned it to his grandmother during their visit yesterday because he'd known there was no way to keep Suzanne out of the conversation. But maybe today she'd be so distracted by Mr. St. Claire, she wouldn't press for details.

Grandmother widened her eyes. "Oh, I've always wanted to go to that. I forgot this was Elvis Week. Being stuck in here has thrown me off." She frowned. "Have you met up with some of your old friends then, dear?"

"I'm having dinner with Ryan tonight," Nick explained. "But other than that, no."

Grandmother raised an eyebrow. "So you went to the Orpheum alone?"

Nick sighed. She could've made a fortune as a private investigator. Or a talk show host. Grandmother's gift for reading people was unmatched. "No. I went with a friend."

Her face broke into a wide smile. "A lady friend?"

"Well yes. She's a lady, and she's my friend. No big deal."

"That's nice, dear." Grandmother smiled knowingly. "You should bring her by sometime."

Nick made a face. He was enjoying his time with Suzanne, that was for sure. But he wasn't about to introduce her to his family. Dinner and a show was one thing, but meeting his grandmother was entirely different. "We'll see." He stood. "Well since it looks like you're in good hands, I think I'm going to try and get some work done before I meet Ryan for dinner tonight." He'd like to at least sketch out his article. Yesterday provided a buffet of characters, from the running Elvises to the baby Elvis he'd seen being pushed in a stroller. He'd even glimpsed a dog with faux sideburns. Definitely fodder for his article. "I'll be back tomorrow. Hopefully the doctor will be able to give us a definitive date for your operation." He leaned down and kissed his grandmother on the cheek.

She patted his hand. "You're getting my mail aren't you? Will you bring it with you tomorrow?"

Nick nodded. "Sure." He turned to Thomas. "It was nice to see you again. Take care." He headed out and pulled the door closed behind him.

After a few hours of work and a nice nap, Nick left his grandmother's house to meet Ryan. He tried to remember the last time they'd seen one another. Must have been sometime while they were in college. Ryan had stayed in Memphis and attended Rhodes College but had driven to Nashville to visit Nick a few times. Then he'd met Lila and hadn't wanted to spend a weekend without her.

Nick pulled into the parking lot at Huey's right on time. A local chain, Huey's had been serving burgers in Memphis since the 1970s. Nick always chose to celebrate his birthday there when he was a boy. He'd loved the tradition of sliding a toothpick into a straw and blowing it up toward the ceiling to try to get it to stick. Years of toothpicks filled the ceiling at Huey's. Nick and Austin used to try to outdo each other and see who could get the most to stick. Sometimes Dad joined in, but Mom would declare their behavior uncouth and lament that she never had a dainty girl. Then she'd laugh and show them all how it was done.

He climbed out of the car and hurried inside. He immediately spotted Ryan sitting in the corner.

Ryan stood, a broad smile on his face. "Hey, man." He pounded Nick on the back. "It's great to see you." Ryan looked almost the same as the day they graduated from high school.

"You, too. It's been forever." Nick settled into the familiar seat and glanced around. "How have you been?"

Ryan grinned. "Life is good. Lila and I are about to celebrate six years in December. And we have two kids. Abby will be five on her next birthday, and Christian turned three yesterday. They keep us busy." He flipped through his smartphone and held up a picture. "This was at the party yesterday."

Nick peered at a photo of a little girl with blond curls who had her arms around an equally blond-haired little boy. "They're adorable." He smiled. "I'm so happy for you." He pushed away an unfamiliar pang of jealousy. He'd never given much thought to having a family of his own, but Ryan's obvious pride in his children made him feel as if he was really missing out.

"I work at the University of Memphis in development, and Lila stays home with the kids. We're doing well," he said.

"Do y'all know what you want yet, or do you need a minute?" the waitress asked.

Nick raised his eyebrows at Ryan.

Ryan nodded. "I think we're ready."

They quickly placed their orders—original Huey burgers, fries, and sweet tea for both of them.

"I'll have your drinks right out," the waitress said with a smile.

"How about you? Seems like you're always on the move," Ryan said.

Nick shrugged. "Yeah, I don't stay in one spot for long."

Ryan furrowed his brow. "That must get old. Don't you ever want to settle down?"

Nick's thoughts automatically flashed to Suzanne. She was the kind of woman he could actually see himself with. Someday. Maybe in ten years. And there was no way she'd still be available then. "I'm not sure. I guess that's one of those things I'll just have to wait and see about."

The waitress set two glasses of tea on the table. "Food will be right out," she said.

Ryan sipped his tea. "Lila has a couple of single girlfriends. I think one is a lawyer and one is a teacher. She's already asked me if you're available for a setup." He raised his eyebrows. "Guess I should tell her no?"

Nick nodded. "Yeah, I don't plan to be here too long." Besides, if he was going to spend time with anyone while he was in Memphis, it would be Suzanne. He might not know where he'd be a year from now, but at least he knew that much.

"So do you see the old gang much?"

Ryan nodded. "We missed you at our five-year reunion. But you know, the ten-year reunion is coming up soon. You think you'll still be here?"

Nick had no desire to come back for a high school reunion. He knew the memory most of his classmates would have of him, and it wasn't one he liked to remember. "Probably not. But e-mail me the details, and I guess if I happen to be in town I could go."

"So you're a writer now," Ryan said. "I ran into your grandmother a few months ago, and she mentioned a few publications your stuff has appeared in. That's awesome."

"Thanks. I enjoy it." He took a sip of tea. "But I don't know that it's what I want to do forever."

The waitress put their plates on the table. "Let me know if you need anything else," she said.

"I'll offer thanks for the food," Ryan said. He said a quick prayer, thanking God for their meal and their friendship. Once he finished he poured ketchup on his plate. "So you don't want to write forever? What do you want to do next?"

Nick shook his head. "I wish I knew. I'd still like to do freelance work for magazines and all, but there are times I think maybe I should find something a little more meaningful." He'd been considering a career change for a few months. The only problem was that he wasn't totally sure he could give up his nomadic lifestyle.

Ryan grinned. "Well if you ever decide to come back to Memphis, my brother-in-law works in HR at St. Jude. It doesn't get more meaningful than that. You might be good in their fund-raising department."

"I'll keep that in mind." The odds of him moving back to Memphis were slim to none, but he didn't want to hurt Ryan's feelings. "I'd forgotten how good these burgers were. Might be the best in the world."

"And you would know," Ryan said with a laugh.

Nick grinned. It was nice to be back with someone who'd known him since before he could write cursive. As much as he'd complained about coming back to Memphis, his time here was turning out to be a real blessing.

eleven

Suzanne checked the clock in the living room. Nick would be here in ten minutes. Just enough time to change out of her work clothes and into something a little more relaxed. She opted for jeans and a red tank top.

She stepped into the bathroom and glanced in the mirror. Not bad. She leaned closer and wiped a smudge of eyeliner out of the corner of her eye. August had been so hot so far that she may as well just give up on wearing makeup. She quickly brushed her teeth and dabbed on a bit of lip gloss. *Ready as I'll ever be.*

The doorbell rang just as she walked into the living room. She opened the door to a smiling Nick.

"Hey," he said, stepping inside. "Thanks for having me over." He held up a bag. "This time I come armed with a variety of treats."

Suzanne laughed. "You're really buttering Charlie up, aren't you?" She motioned toward the kitchen. "He's out back right now. I figured it would be easier to keep him outside until the pizza got here, otherwise we'd have to endure a lot of barking and general mayhem."

"Well I'm totally against mayhem." He grinned. "Can I go out back and give him a treat now?"

"Sure." She led him through the dining room to the kitchen.

He paused at the refrigerator and surveyed the hodgepodge

of pictures and notes displayed there. "Is this you graduating from college?" he asked pointing at a picture.

She walked over to see which one he was looking at. "Oh yeah." She laughed. "That's me and Grandpa on the day I graduated. He was so proud."

"What a great picture." His eyes fell on a dry-erase board with a Bible verse written on it: *"'For I know the plans I have for you,' declares the Lord, 'plans to prosper you and not to harm you, plans to give you hope and a future.'" Jeremiah 29:11.* He glanced at Suzanne. "Favorite verse?"

She shook her head. "It's this thing I've been doing for the past few years. I find a verse that I really need to apply to my life and write it up there." She smiled. "Most of the time, I leave them up for just a week or two before I change."

"How long has this one been up?"

She met his brown-eyed gaze. "Two months. I guess you could say that trusting in the Lord's plan for my life is a challenge for me."

Nick nodded. "It's hard for everyone, I think."

"I know that there have been opportunities I've been given that I've been too scared to take. I always think I should take a leap of faith and see what He has in store for me, but fear holds me back."

"What's the latest one?"

You. She held back the word. "My rental house is going up for sale at the end of next month. So I either have to find a new place to rent or decide to become a homeowner."

"So what's holding you back?"

She opened the refrigerator and took out two bottles of water. She handed one to him and opened the other. "That seems awfully final, don't you think? I'm just not sure I'm ready for that kind of commitment."

Nick nodded. "It is a big decision. But buying a home isn't a prison. You can always sell it or rent it out if you decide it isn't what you want. Right?"

She took a swig of water. "I know you're right. But in my mind that's the kind of thing I want to be certain of. I really don't want to make a mistake and wind up somewhere I don't really want to be." Although she had to admit, Saturday night when she'd crashed after the 5K, she'd gotten sucked into a marathon of HGTV. The prospect of having her own space to decorate and landscape however she wanted felt kind of exciting.

"So you think this is one of those things that could be part of God's plan for your life?"

She shrugged. "All I know is that whenever things seem to fall into place easily, I always get the feeling that I should pay attention. You know?"

"I sure do. That's part of what brought me back to Memphis. My lease happened to be up in Atlanta at the same time my grandmother was going into the hospital. And since I wasn't sure where I wanted to go next, it seemed like Memphis was where I was supposed to be."

She twisted her mouth into a smile. "And is it?"

"For now. Especially for right now in this moment."

Something about the way he looked at her made her pulse race. A little more intensity glimmered in his eyes tonight.

The doorbell rang, breaking the moment. "I'll get it. You give Charlie his treat." She grabbed some cash off the coffee table and answered the door.

The pizza delivery girl stood on the porch with a grin, holding two large pizzas. "Hi," she said.

Suzanne smiled and handed her the cash. "Keep the change."

The girl nodded, her red ponytail bobbing. "Thank you." She handed the hot pizzas to Suzanne.

Suzanne put the pizzas on the coffee table and went out into the backyard. "Everything okay out here?" Nick sat in one of the patio chairs, and Charlie was engrossed in his bone.

"We're good. Hungry though." Nick grinned.

"Well, come on then."

They settled on the couch, and Nick opened the pizzas. "A large cheese and a large pepperoni. Good call," he said.

Suzanne took a bite. "Delicious."

They ate in silence for a moment.

"So is Elvis Week over now?" Nick asked.

She shook her head. "Nope. One more big event to go. The big finale." She smiled. "Tomorrow night is the candlelight vigil. Thousands of people will line up with candles and walk to Elvis's grave. It's actually very somber and kind of beautiful."

Nick widened his eyes. "How long does it last?"

"I think it starts when the sun goes down and lasts all night. Or until the last person makes it to the grave. I'm talking a lot of people, so it takes quite a long time." She tossed the last of her crust onto her plate. She glanced up to see Nick staring at her. "What?"

He put his plate on the coffee table then took her plate and set it on the coffee table. He reached up and brushed her lip with his thumb. "You have just a little sauce there."

"If this was a movie. . ." She trailed off.

Nick grinned. He stood up and held out a hand to her.

She took his hand, and he pulled her toward him until they were face-to-face.

"I wanted to do this the other night when I brought you home, but I wouldn't let myself. And then when I walked you to the car after the 5K, I fought every instinct I had."

She knew she should back away. Go check on Charlie or scoop some ice cream into a bowl. But she stood, rooted to the spot. Because she'd wanted the same thing he had.

Nick leaned down and kissed her softly on the mouth.

She leaned into him, delighting in the feel of his lips on hers.

He pulled away with a grin. "Just like I thought it would be."

"Awful," she said, her voice glum.

They burst out laughing. The kiss had been anything but awful. In fact, if Suzanne had to describe the perfect first kiss, that would've been it.

Nick pulled her to him and kissed her again, but this time on the forehead. "Now that we have that out of the way, we can relax."

"I was relaxed," she said with a laugh.

He grinned. "Well I was a little nervous. I almost kissed you earlier in the kitchen, but we were discussing a Bible verse, and it didn't seem quite right." He chuckled.

She shook her head at him. "You're too much. I'm going to let Charlie in. Why don't you put the pizza in the fridge?"

"And then?" He raised his eyebrows. "What do you have in mind after that?"

"Simple, Mr. Competitive. We go Wii bowling to see who has to buy dinner next time."

His laughter followed her out the back door. Once she

stepped outside, she tried to get her heart to stop pounding. Most of her long-distance relationships had been free of kissing. So it wasn't like she was super-experienced in that department. But she knew enough to know that whatever was brewing between her and Nick had real feelings behind it.

And even though she was glad he'd kissed her, she couldn't help but wonder how much harder they'd just made their inevitable good-bye.

❧

The next night, Nick waited in line with what seemed like a million other people at the gates of Graceland. If he thought the Elvis tribute contest drew a wild crowd, it was nothing compared to this. He'd lost track of the number of languages he'd overheard.

Between the people, the candles, and the media trucks, it was quite a scene. Nick pulled out a small notepad and jotted down some notes. He'd talked to a few people who made the trek yearly and others who were here for the first time. It seemed like everyone had an Elvis story.

The woman behind him had offered her opinion: "His music got me through some tough times, especially his gospel albums. I don't know if there is a sweeter sound than Elvis's version of 'Amazing Grace.' I played it for my babies when they were fussy, and they'd calm right down. And we played it at Mama's funeral. And someday, it will be played at mine. His music is timeless; that's what it is."

The wide variety of ages represented in the line surprised Nick. He'd expected a mostly older crowd, but he discovered a mix. Clearly, whatever it was that Elvis had possessed, it crossed generational lines even years after his death.

Nick finished making his notes and shoved the notepad back in the pocket of his cargo shorts. He'd stayed busy all day, but whenever he grew still he found himself going over last night again in his mind. The way Suzanne's lips felt against his might just be the best feeling in the world. And after that, they'd laughed so much, playing Wii tennis and bowling. Charlie had jumped up and barked every now and then, adding to the chaos.

Once she had solidly beaten him two out of three games, they'd collapsed on the couch and watched an old episode of *The Cosby Show* before he left to go home.

Nick kissed her one more time at the door, and he couldn't help but realize their evening—of pizza, conversation, and laughter—was the kind of normal night they could have if they lived in the same place. For just a split second, he'd longed for that kind of life. The kind where he came home from work and his house wasn't empty.

He quickly pushed the thought away. His judgment had clearly been clouded by their kiss.

"You a big Elvis fan?" the guy in front of him asked, jolting him back to the present.

Nick grinned. "I definitely like some of his music. And no one can argue with his star power. It's somehow still magnetic even decades after his death." Nick pulled out his notepad. "I'd love to ask you some questions if you don't mind."

The guy nodded. "Sure."

Focus on work. Not Suzanne. "Tell me about your earliest memory of Elvis." Nick put his pen on the paper and waited for the guy to respond. If it kept his mind off Suzanne, he'd talk to every person in this line.

twelve

Suzanne leaned back at her desk at work and rubbed her temples. "Have I mentioned how glad I am that Elvis Week is officially over?" she asked.

Avis giggled. "Girl, me, too. I mean, no week is totally normal around here, but I felt like I was living in some kind of crazy world lately."

Suzanne nodded. "No doubt. I'll be glad to just work on run-of-the-mill weddings and the occasional after-hours event." She grinned.

"So what did you decide to do about your house? Are you joining the ranks of us homeowners?"

Suzanne let out a huge sigh. "I don't know yet. I went ahead and got preapproved for a mortgage just in case I decide to buy. But I haven't actually done any house hunting yet."

"Baby steps." Avis burst into laughter. "I'm impressed that you're even considering it. I think you could be really happy with your own place."

Suzanne's eyes twinkled . "I'm ashamed to admit this, but I've started watching HGTV lately. And now I'm hooked." Because she'd always been a renter, Suzanne had never upgraded from her college-style furniture. She had a hodgepodge of things she'd picked up at thrift stores over the years. The idea of decorating her own place thrilled her.

Avis squealed. "You're getting house fever." She smiled

broadly. "That's better than baby fever. Not nearly as expensive, and you can sell the house when it starts giving you fits."

"That's one way to look at things," Suzanne said. She glanced at the clock on her computer. "Okay. I'm out of here. Hope you have a wonderful weekend."

"You, too," Avis called.

Suzanne hadn't seen Nick since the night they kissed. She'd talked to him on the phone a few times though. He'd taken his grandmother home yesterday. After all the delays caused by her blood pressure, her doctor went out of town. His grandmother had insisted on going home for the weekend, and the surgery was scheduled for next week.

Suzanne headed toward her house. Traffic wasn't as bad as normal for a Friday afternoon. Must be a lot of people out of town for one last summer hurrah.

Nick invited her to dinner tonight, but he wasn't supposed to pick her up until a little before seven. Which would give her some time to relax. She pulled into the driveway and went inside.

Charlie met her at the door, his favorite stuffed bunny in his mouth.

She reached down and tugged on the bunny.

Charlie tugged back. Tug-of-war was his favorite game. He wasn't much of a fetcher, but he loved to tug.

Suzanne eased into the patio chair and scratched Charlie behind the ears. She'd lived in six different places in Memphis. Was it time to make the city her permanent home? "Come on, boy. Let's go inside."

Charlie trotted along behind her and went straight for the water bowl.

Suzanne slipped on a pair of dark jeans and a pink flutter-sleeve top. She paired the outfit with her favorite wedge heels, thankful her calves had healed from her recent run. She and Nick were going to dinner at Houston's and then planned to catch a movie at the drive-in theater on Summer Avenue. She'd grown to love the drive-in since she moved to Memphis. It was only open on weekends and played a double feature.

The doorbell rang.

Suzanne glanced in the full-length mirror at the end of the hallway. Not bad, considering she felt totally exhausted. She hoped she wouldn't fall asleep during the movie.

She flung open the door. "Hey," she said.

Nick grinned. "Ready?"

She nodded and followed him out to his grandmother's car. "Now that your grandmother is home from the hospital, does she want her car back?"

He laughed and started the engine. "Oh yeah. I thought she was going to flip out tonight when she found out I was going out and taking the car. I don't know where she thought she was going. The doctor doesn't want her to do much of anything except rest."

"So the surgery is rescheduled?"

"Wednesday."

"She must be relieved to finally have a solid date." She looked over at Nick. "And you too, right? That means you're that much closer to getting out of Memphis."

The words hung between them for a long moment.

"I feel like I'm in limbo here," he confessed. "So in that respect, it will be nice to get back to normal." He laughed. "Whatever that is."

He pulled into the parking lot at Houston's. "I haven't been here in forever. I hope it's as good as I remember."

"Oh, it is. This is definitely one of my favorite places."

Nick's phone buzzed. He held it up and checked the caller ID. "It's my grandmother." He shot Suzanne a worried glance. "I'd better take it. She insisted I go out tonight but promised she'd call if she needed me."

She stared out the window trying to guess which couples were established and which ones were on a first date based on their body language.

Nick clicked the phone off and sighed.

"Trouble?" she asked.

"She wants us to come to her house. Says she isn't feeling great and doesn't want to be alone." He raised his eyebrows at her. "I can just take you home though."

Suzanne shook her head. "Don't be silly. I'll go with you. Maybe she'll feel better, and we can at least catch the late show."

Nick hesitated. "You don't mind?"

"No. Let's go. We can drive through and grab dinner or just order pizza again."

He turned on Poplar Avenue and headed toward Germantown. "My grandmother will probably grill you. I'm just giving you fair warning."

Suzanne laughed. "It's fine."

Fifteen minutes later, they pulled up in front of a giant house. If this were the kind of home Suzanne was in the market for, her decision would be easy. It was beautiful. "Wow," she whispered. This was a very expensive home in a very expensive neighborhood. She hadn't gotten a spoiled-rich-kid vibe from

Nick, but suddenly his world traveling made more sense. He must not be living solely on a freelancing salary. She followed Nick up the sidewalk and into the foyer.

"Grandmother? We're here," he called.

"I'm in the library."

Nick guided Suzanne through a living room and a formal dining room and stopped in a large room filled with floor-to-ceiling bookshelves. "Grandmother, this is my friend Suzanne."

Suzanne stepped forward and offered a hand to the elderly woman perched on a chaise lounge.

Nick's grandmother smiled at her and shook her hand. "It's so nice to finally meet you, Suzanne. I'm pleased that Nicholas made a friend to spend time with while he's here visiting." She patted the end of the lounger. "Sit here and tell me about yourself."

Suzanne sat down and looked up at Nick. He didn't look pleased.

"Nicholas, why don't you get us a snack and some water?" his grandmother asked.

Nick nodded. "Be right back." He shot a look at Suzanne and hurried off.

"So, Suzanne. Nicholas hasn't told me too much about you."

Suzanne frowned. At least his grandmother was honest, but that wasn't exactly what she wanted to hear.

"But even so, I can see that you mean a lot to him. He doesn't talk as much about catching the next flight out of town as he did when he first got here. And I can't help but think that you might have something to do with that." She smiled, and her blue eyes twinkled. "That's the real reason I asked you two to come here tonight. I wanted some time alone with you."

"I don't know, Mrs. Taggart; I'm pretty sure Nick still plans on hitting the road as soon as you're well."

Mrs. Taggart nodded. "Of course. But the urge to leave isn't as strong as it was when he first got here. I don't know what Nicholas has told you about his past, but he's been through a lot. It's not my story to tell, so I'll let him do that in his own time." She reached out and grasped Suzanne's hand. "But I think you could be really good for him. He's been on his own for so long." She shook her head. "I guess I'm hoping that you will be a reason for him to stay here."

No pressure or anything. Suzanne shook her head. "We're having a nice time together, but I really don't believe his plans include Memphis."

"Maybe not. But maybe there are bigger plans in the works here," Mrs. Taggart said softly. "I've been praying for that boy to finally make peace with his past ever since he was seventeen. I'm hopeful that this is finally the year he'll do that."

Nick walked into the room carrying a tray with some cheese and crackers and three bottled waters. He set the tray on the coffee table. "Here you go." He glanced uneasily from Suzanne to his grandmother. "Did I miss something?"

Suzanne shook her head. "Just getting to know your grandmother." She flashed the woman a smile. She couldn't help but wonder what had happened to Nick when he was seventeen. But it sounded like she'd just have to wait until he was ready to talk about it before she could find out.

❧

Monday afternoon Nick sat in the driveway at Suzanne's house. He'd just taken his grandmother back to the hospital and was supposed to meet Suzanne here after work. Since they'd missed dinner the other night, they were going to try again.

It had ended up being a fun night though. Suzanne and Grandmother had gotten along really well, and the three of them played old board games until his grandmother went to bed.

Most of the women he'd gone out with would've been irritated to give up dinner at Houston's for board games and snack food with an elderly woman, but Suzanne had a wonderful time. And he could tell that she'd won his grandmother over, too. Before she'd retired to the bedroom, Grandmother had asked Suzanne to join them for lunch one Sunday as soon as she recovered from her surgery. He'd known then that Suzanne had two fans in the Taggart family.

He watched her Pathfinder pull up into the driveway next to him.

She smiled and climbed out of the vehicle. "You're early," she chided.

Nick shrugged. "I wanted to see you?"

"Was there a question mark at the end of that?" she asked with a laugh.

"Well, I'm early because I was tired of sitting at the hospital, and I didn't want to drive all the way out to Germantown and then back here." He grinned. "But I did want to see you, too."

"Whatever. It's all about convenience for you. I see how you are." She motioned for him to follow her to the porch. She stuck the key in the lock. "Now beware. Charlie will probably not like that you're with me. He's used to having me all to himself when I get home."

"And here I am without a single dog bone to use as a bribe. I knew I forgot something."

Suzanne opened the door and walked in.

Charlie stood right inside holding a toy in his mouth.

Nick grabbed the toy and tossed it into the yard. "Get it." He stepped back and watched as Charlie dashed into the yard. And kept on running.

"What were you thinking?" Suzanne asked angrily, brushing past him. "He's not the kind of dog that goes out unless it's fenced."

Nick stood, frozen, and watched as Suzanne ran full speed after Charlie. For an older dog, he sure was fast. *This might end badly for me and for Charlie.* Nick grabbed the keys from the door and picked up Suzanne's purse from where she'd dropped it as she ran.

He hurried to the car and set off after them, praying silently as he drove.

thirteen

Suzanne ran so fast her lungs burned. "Charlie!" she screamed.

The dog kept running. He'd stop to relieve himself on a tree and sniff the ground around every bush he came to, but as soon as Suzanne drew close, he'd take off again.

"Charlie, stop!" Suzanne kept screaming. *Please let him be okay. Please let me catch him.*

Neighbors stepped out onto their porches as her screams alerted them. "Don't chase him. Just kneel down, and he'll come to you," one lady called.

Suzanne glared. That might work for some dogs, but Charlie would see her kneeling down as his chance to escape. She rounded the corner in time to see him start to dart across White Station Road. It was a busy four-lane road, and there were cars everywhere. "Stop, please stop!" she yelled. She tried waving her hands at motorists to signal them to slow down, but the cars kept whizzing past.

She looked toward the blare of a horn and the sickening screech of tires just in time to see a car hit her beloved Charlie.

"No!" She ran blindly into the road as angry drivers honked and yelled obscenities at her out their windows.

She reached the far lane just as the driver of the stopped car scrambled out, but she didn't pay him any attention.

Charlie lay still, but his eyes locked on hers. He whimpered when he saw her.

"Sweet boy," she sank onto her knees and stroked his fur. "You're going to be okay. You have to be okay." She sobbed. What if he wasn't going to be okay?

"I'm so sorry, miss. He came out of nowhere." The shaken teenage boy knelt down next to her. "Can I call someone?"

She couldn't form words. She stared blankly at the boy. Call someone?

"Help me get him into the car," Nick commanded softly.

She turned and saw that Nick had pulled up next to them. The horns blaring behind them as they clogged up two lanes of traffic seemed very far away.

"Be careful," she whispered.

Nick and the teenager gently lifted Charlie from the road and laid him in the backseat of Nick's grandmother's car.

Suzanne turned away from the sound of Charlie's whimpers. Clearly moving him had caused him more pain.

Nick walked over and helped Suzanne to her feet. "Come on. We need to get him to the vet." He guided her into the backseat next to Charlie.

"Eastgate Animal Clinic," she whispered. "That's our vet and the closest one to where we are."

Nick nodded silently. "I know where it is."

Her tears fell onto Charlie's fur. She stroked his head.

The dog's big brown eyes never strayed from her face.

"It will be okay," she whispered. "I love you."

After what seemed like hours but must've only been minutes, Nick eased the car to a stop. "Stay here with him. I'll go inside to tell them what's going on, and they'll come bring him in." He slammed the door and ran inside.

"Please, Charlie. Please be okay." A loud sob caught in her

throat. She wiped her eyes and wished for a tissue.

Nick opened the door, the vet and a vet tech with him.

"We'll take it from here," the vet said. He and the tech carefully loaded Charlie onto a stretcher and carried him inside.

Nick leaned into the car and offered his hand. "Do you want to wait inside or out here?"

She shook her head. She didn't know. Her whole body felt numb. "Are there people in the waiting room?"

"No." He grasped her hand. "How about we go in and see if they can get you some water? You look pale."

She furrowed her brow. "You think? I just watched my dog, who has been with me for more than ten years, get hit by a car. Of course I look pale." She couldn't keep the anger out of her voice. This wasn't fair. Charlie hadn't done anything to deserve to be hit.

"I know. Come on in, and we'll see if there's any news."

She let him guide her out of the car and into the building.

The receptionist jumped up when they went inside and handed her some tissue. "I'm so sorry, Suzanne. They're working on Charlie now."

"Can you get her some water?" Nick asked.

The girl nodded. "Of course. I'll be right back."

Nick led Suzanne over to a blue plastic chair. He gripped her hand tightly. "Come here." He pulled her against him, and she stiffened.

"What were you thinking?" Suzanne pulled away from him.

"I'm so sorry. I didn't know he'd run off."

Suzanne angrily wiped her eyes. "Charlie is all I have. He's been there for me when no one else was. And now. . ." She trailed off as her tears fell in earnest. She knew it was irrational for her to be angry with Nick. But if he'd been more careful, none of this would've happened.

Nick raked his fingers through his hair. "I wasn't thinking. It was stupid of me." He took her hand. "You know I never would've done something like that on purpose. The last thing in the world I ever want to do is cause you pain."

Suzanne nodded. "I know." She squeezed his hand.

He pulled her to him again, and this time she let him hold her.

As she leaned against his chest, a sob caught in her throat. "I'm glad you're here," she whispered. "I wouldn't want to do this alone."

"Shh." He smoothed her hair. "I'm glad I'm here, too."

He held on to her for what seemed like hours.

Suzanne kept her eyes closed, trying to block out her surroundings. She'd been bringing Charlie here since he was just a puppy.

The door to the back finally opened, and Nick nudged her.

She opened her eyes and saw the doctor standing in the doorway, a grim expression on his face. She jumped up. "Is he okay?"

The doctor sighed. "We did everything we could do. He's alive, but barely. I'll be honest with you, Suzanne. I don't know if he'll pull through or not. We'll know more tomorrow. If he makes it through the night, I'd say he has a good chance. But there was some internal bleeding, and one of his legs is broken." He reached out and clasped her hands. "We did the best we could do."

Suzanne swallowed as a new round of tears began to fall.

"So there's a chance that he'll be okay, right?"

The vet nodded. "Like I said, if he makes it through the night I'd say his odds are good. But these next few hours are critical." He glanced at Nick. "There's nothing more you can do here. I'll monitor him overnight. If anything changes, I'll call."

"Thanks," she whispered. She leaned against Nick and let him lead her out to the car.

They rode in silence back to her house.

Suzanne glanced down and realized Nick must've grabbed her purse for her after she took off running. It had been a long time since someone had cared for her during a crisis. Over the past years, she'd gotten so used to taking care of everything herself, she'd forgotten what it was like to lean on someone. "Thanks for grabbing my purse," she said.

He glanced over at her, a worried expression on his face. "You dropped it in the driveway. I don't think you even realized it." He pulled the car into her driveway and parked behind her SUV. He killed the engine and peered over at her. "Do you want to be left alone? Or can I come inside for a while?"

She managed a tiny smile. "Please come in with me." She reached into her purse and fumbled for the keys. She unlocked the door, and they walked inside. Her eyes landed on Charlie's dog bed in the corner. It was where he slept during the day. At night he slept at the foot of her bed. Most mornings, Charlie woke her up by sitting up and staring at her until she opened her eyes. "It's weird to be here and him not be at my feet."

Nick shook his head. "I know." He motioned toward the couch. "Sit down, and I'll get you something to drink."

She sank onto the couch next to one of Charlie's stuffed

animals. He lugged those things everywhere, and most of them were missing eyes and noses by now. She picked the stuffed bunny up, and fresh tears sprang into her eyes.

"Here you go," Nick said, walking into the living room with two glasses of tea.

She took a glass from him and sipped it slowly. "Thanks."

"Listen, I'm so sorry. This is all my fault." Nick sat down next to her. "I didn't realize he would run off like that. I just thought he would do his business and come back inside."

She shook her head. The anger she'd felt toward Nick earlier had subsided. She knew it had been an accident. "You couldn't know. I guess I never mentioned to you that Charlie is a runner." She took another sip of tea. "He got out once a few years ago, and ever since he had that tiny taste of freedom, he's been intrigued by life outside of the fence. Of course, that was in my hometown, so there wasn't much traffic. Grandpa and I were able to chase him down in the pickup truck, and Charlie hopped up in the cab with us once we found him. Since then, I've been super paranoid about him getting out."

"Well, I'm still sorry. I feel awful."

She reached over and took his hand. "Stop apologizing." She liked the way their hands looked joined together. Having him here was quite comforting. "He's going to be okay, isn't he? I mean, the fact that he came through surgery and all has to be a good sign, right?"

Nick pressed his lips together. He reached over and brushed a strand of hair from her eyes. "I don't think you should get your hopes up. Sometimes these things happen and they can't be helped."

She furrowed her brow and jerked her hand away. "That's

not exactly what I wanted to hear."

"I'm just saying that in my experience, these things don't always turn out well. No matter how much you hope or how much you pray. Sometimes you have to just let go."

She drew back like she'd been slapped. "I intend to hold out hope until the doctor tells me otherwise. I thought you'd do the same."

Nick sighed. "I just want you to be realistic. And I don't want you to be devastated tomorrow."

Anger raged inside Suzanne. All she wanted was a little support from him. Even if he didn't think everything was going to be okay, he could at least pretend. "What is wrong with you?"

"It's the cycle of life. No one—not a person or an animal—lives forever."

She glared. "I'm aware of the cycle of life, Nick. For your information, I lost my grandpa three months ago to cancer. So I'm well aware that things don't always work out. But there's nothing wrong with holding on to a little hope at a time like this."

Nick stood and began to pace. "I haven't told you this before, but my parents and brother were killed in an accident a few years ago. I clung to hope, too, and it made it that much harder when the outcome wasn't what I wanted it to be. I just don't want you to have more pain than you have to have."

Suzanne froze. Why had he chosen this moment to share that information with her? She'd asked him early on about his parents, and he hadn't mentioned their accident. "I'm sorry to hear that, Nick." At least now she knew what his grandmother was alluding to the other night.

"I shouldn't have mentioned it. It's in the past," he said.

"It explains a lot though," she mumbled under her breath, more to herself than to him.

"What did you just say?" he asked.

She knew she should just keep her mouth shut. But a part of her was angry with him for choosing this point in time to tell her something so personal, especially when he'd had ample opportunity before. She leveled her gaze on him. "Just that it explains a lot about you. About why you keep people at an arm's length. Why you have that giant wall up around yourself." She shook her head. "Why you don't form attachments to anyone anywhere except for casual acquaintances. Not even to a pet."

Nick stopped pacing and turned to face her. "So you've got me all figured out, huh?"

Suzanne stood and strode over to him until they were face-to-face. "It makes sense to me."

His eyes blazed, but she didn't care. He could hide behind his pain if he wanted to, but he wasn't going to take away her hope that Charlie would be okay.

❧

The intense guilt Nick felt over Charlie's accident was reminiscent of the guilt he'd carried with him for years over his parents' accident. He knew deep down that neither of them was his fault, but that didn't lessen the pain.

"Well then tell me. . . If that's my problem, what's yours? You're just as bad as me with your long-distance relationships and your fear of putting down permanent roots. And, by the way, your wall is almost as big as mine. And just as tough to get through."

She blinked, and for a moment he thought she might cry.

He shouldn't even have mentioned the accident. Suzanne was clearly in shock over watching Charlie get hit. She was in no shape to digest the information right now. But he'd wanted her to realize that loss was a part of life. It had been a hard lesson for him, and he'd wanted to make it easier for her. Clearly he'd gone about it the wrong way.

Suzanne composed herself and lifted her chin defiantly. "Fine. 'You show me your wound, and I'll show you mine.' Is that what this is?" she asked. "My dad left us when I was ten. Not in a share custody, we-see-each-other-on-holidays way either. But in an 'I don't want to be married and don't want the responsibility of fatherhood' way. He just left. I haven't seen him since." She took a breath. "My mother was broken. Broken. She never bounced back, and in some ways, I didn't either. I vowed then and there that no man would ever make me feel that way again—unwanted, like I wasn't worth his time. So yeah, I push people away. I keep them at a distance. And I'm terrified at the thought of settling down with someone who might decide next week or next year that he just doesn't want that lifestyle anymore."

He wanted to reach out to her but stopped himself. The fire in her eyes told him that she didn't want to be touched, especially by him. "I'm sorry. That must've been tough on you." He sighed. "But at least your dad is still alive."

Her eyes flashed. "You really have a knack for saying the wrong thing, don't you?"

Nick raked his fingers through his hair. What had he said? "It's the truth. I just mean that at least your dad is still around."

She shook her head. "You don't get it. This is not a competition. We're not competing to see which of us has had the worst experience. What you went through was awful. I can't imagine losing your family like that. And what I went through was awful, too. A different kind of awful. My dad *chose* to leave me. He *chooses* every day to not be part of my life. The experiences you and I have gone through are both horrible, but this isn't a competition." She wrapped her arms around herself. "I think you should just leave."

"Just like that."

She nodded. "Just like that. We aren't going to see eye to eye on anything right now. I just want to get in bed and hope that tomorrow brings good news about Charlie. And I'm going to hang on to that glimmer of hope until I have a reason not to." She opened the front door.

Nick brushed past her. This day had started out with a lot of promise. And had ended terribly. "Please call me tomorrow and let me know how Charlie is doing," he said softly.

She nodded.

He walked out to his grandmother's Lexus and headed toward Germantown. He hadn't meant to upset her and then continue to upset her. He should've just kept his mouth shut. *You're really on a roll.*

fourteen

Suzanne hadn't slept at all last night. She'd sat up worrying about Charlie and thinking about Nick and what he'd shared about his family's accident. She hadn't wanted to argue with him. And from the expression on his face, she was nearly certain he hadn't wanted to be in an argument either.

She poured a cup of coffee and went into the living room. She'd already called her office to let them know she was taking a personal day today. She rarely took a day off but felt like the events of yesterday and the possibility of today justified it. She glanced at the wall clock. The vet's office should be opening now. She turned her phone over and over in her hand. Once she called, there was no turning back. Right now, at this moment, she could believe the best. But once she placed the call, the news could be devastating.

It was like that country song—she couldn't remember who sang it—about the guy who wished he didn't know now what he didn't know then. Once you found out the truth about something, there was no undoing it. You had to deal with the news. She sighed and leaned against the couch.

If Charlie hadn't made it through the night, she would be devastated. The pain would be horrible. But she would move forward, and eventually she would probably get another pet. The new pet wouldn't take Charlie's place but would find its own place in her life. And she'd have a decade of memories of Charlie.

Armed with that resolve, she hit the button and dialed the vet's office.

Busy.

"Great." She paced the length of the living room. She'd give it a minute and call again.

The doorbell rang.

Suzanne peeked through the peephole. Nick stood on the other side of the door.

She cracked the door. "What are you doing here?" She hadn't expected to see him today. After the way she'd acted yesterday, she'd figured he might need some space.

The dark circles under his eyes told her he hadn't slept any better than she had. "Can I come inside?"

She nodded. "Of course."

He stepped inside and closed the door behind him.

Suzanne spoke first. "Sorry about yesterday. I know I probably wasn't very sympathetic about your parents and brother. I'm very sorry for all that you've gone through."

Nick pressed his lips together. "It was the wrong time to drop that bomb on you. You were already processing enough without me adding to it." His face brightened. "But I have good news for you. I just dropped by Eastgate and spoke to the vet. Charlie is still hanging in there. The vet is pleased."

She widened her eyes. "You did? He is?" Relief washed over her. The knot that had twisted her stomach since yesterday afternoon started to unravel.

"I hope you don't mind. I didn't think you should be alone if it was bad news, and then when it was good news. . . I wanted to come by and tell you myself." He flashed her a small smile. "The vet said he's doing much better today and that if you want to come by and see him later that will be fine. He'll have to stay there for a few more days though."

"Of course." Suzanne suddenly realized that she must look awful. She hadn't even glanced in a mirror this morning, and her yoga pants and T-shirt wouldn't win her any awards. But she knew Nick didn't care.

He cleared his throat. "I want to explain a few things to you if that's okay."

She nodded. "Have a seat."

They settled down on the couch, and she clutched her coffee.

"When I was in high school, I was really good at football," he started. "I had scouts looking at me from the time I was a freshman. I was the quarterback for our team, just like my dad had been."

She set her coffee down on the coffee table and met his eyes. "You don't have to do this."

"I need to. I want you to know the whole story."

She nodded.

He drew a deep breath. "My parents were so proud, especially Dad. He'd blown out his knee his senior year and never played college ball. So I guess he always thought I'd get to live out his dream." He shrugged. "Of course, it was my dream, too."

She'd been able to tell he was athletic from the moment they met, so his story made sense.

"My brother, Austin, was two years younger than me. We were best friends, but he'd always looked up to me, you know? My junior year had just started, and he was a freshman. It was the Friday night of our game against our biggest in-town rivals." He pressed his lips together as if gathering strength. "I guess Austin had gotten in my bag of gear and had taken out my jersey. He was probably wearing it around. He did that sometimes. But that time, he forgot to put it back in my bag."

She could see where this was going and didn't want to know the rest. The pain in his eyes was so great, she didn't want to have to hear him speak the words. But she knew he had to say them.

"I got to the locker room and realized I didn't have my jersey. I was so hyped up. I'd been looking forward to that game since the previous season when they'd beaten us. Plus there was going to be a scout there from the University of Alabama. That's where I wanted to play."

She'd played sports growing up, so she knew how it felt just before a big game.

"I was so mad. I called home, and Austin answered. I let him have it about my jersey, and when he put Mom on the phone, I argued with her, too, and she told me I'd have to just start out wearing one that was at school and change at halftime. She said there was no way she'd have time to bring my jersey to me before we started warm-ups because she was making snacks for the team's after-game party." He shook his head. "I wanted that one though, because it was my lucky jersey. I'd won the past two games wearing it, and I didn't want to take a chance. But I went ahead and put the other one on and started warming up." He picked up the remote from the coffee table and began turning it over and over in his hands. "I guess Mom felt bad because all three of them loaded up in Dad's car to bring the jersey in time for me to change for game time. They were going through the stoplight at Park and Ridgeway when a drunk driver hit them. The guy didn't even try to stop. He just plowed into them." He wiped his eyes. "Dad was driving and was killed instantly. Mom and Austin were rushed to the hospital in critical condition. Both were unconscious."

Suzanne let out a breath she hadn't realized she was holding. "Nick, I'm so sorry."

He nodded but continued. "My grandmother found out first and called my coach. She insisted that no one tell me. She wanted me to have one more night of normalcy before I learned the news. Plus there was nothing I could do at that point. It wasn't like any of them would even know I was there." He put the remote back in its spot. "We won the game. It was the last time I remember being totally whole. As soon as the clock ticked down and we celebrated at midfield, my coach came and told me to go get in his car instead of going to the locker room. He broke the news and took me straight to the hospital where my grandparents were waiting."

"Your grandparents?" She'd only heard him speak of his grandmother up until this point.

He nodded. "My grandfather was in poor health at the time. He didn't last much longer. Dad was an only child, and the two of them were great friends. I think it was just too much for him to take." He sighed. "Anyway, by the time I made it to the hospital, Mom had died in surgery. Austin was on life support, but there wasn't any brain activity. He died two days later."

"You blamed yourself," she said quietly. She could see it on his face.

He nodded. "How could I not? I was such a brat thinking I was some hotshot football star who was invincible. If I'd just been mature and not made a big deal about Austin wearing my jersey, none of it would've happened."

She reached over and took his hand. "You were as mature

as any other kid in high school. You were just a kid. It wasn't your fault." She shook her head. "You know that now, right?"

He shrugged. "I was selfish. And that selfishness impacted my whole family, my whole life. I moved in with my grandparents and never stepped foot on the football field again. My coach thought I'd come back for my senior season, but I didn't have the heart. It had been something Dad and I shared, and without him I didn't want to experience it anymore."

"And all that is why you haven't been back to Memphis."

Nick nodded. "I kept thinking if I could just get far enough away, I'd forget. But the memories catch up eventually, no matter what city I'm in. I'll be in Los Angeles, and a show will come on TV that's set in Memphis. Or I'll be in Chicago, and I'll hear a snippet of Elvis. Even overseas, I'll see a father and son throwing a football in the park." He shook his head. "You can run from your past, but you can't hide."

"You're right. You can try, but you won't succeed." How many years had she spent running from the ghost of her parents' marriage? And how close had she come to allowing that to control the rest of her life? "I'm glad you told me the whole story. It helps me to understand you better." A dull ache spread through Suzanne's chest. She feared that no matter how well she understood him or how close she got to him, it wouldn't be enough. Even though he might attempt to face his past, that didn't mean he would be able to change the man he'd turned into.

Nick may never want to have a real relationship with anyone. Including her.

❧

Nick felt as though a huge weight had lifted from his shoulders.

"You're the only person I've ever told that story to, which is why it came as somewhat of a surprise yesterday when I blurted it out. I've traveled all over the world, and when pressed, I just say that my family was killed in an accident. I've never gone into detail until now, with you." He squeezed her hand. "Thank you for letting me unload on you." She probably didn't realize it, but the fact that he felt comfortable enough to open up to her was huge for him. It made him happy and terrified him at the same time.

"I'm glad you told me. I know that talking about painful things from the past isn't easy, especially for people like us who seem to internalize everything."

He nodded. They were similar in that way. "I'm sorry about yesterday. I didn't mean to give you the impression that I was trying to compete with you over who'd had the most traumatic childhood." He sighed. "We all have our own burdens to bear, I guess. I can't imagine what it must've been like for you when your dad left."

Suzanne nodded. "It hurt then, and it hurts now. I've finally accepted that no matter how old I am, the fact that my own father didn't love me enough to stick around or stay in touch with me will always cause me pain."

"I don't even know how you begin to deal with that."

She shook her head. "My grandpa really stepped up. He did all the stuff a dad was supposed to do. Moved me into the college dorm. Made sure the oil in my car got changed. Grilled my prom date." She gave him a tiny smile. "So it wasn't like my life was all bad. I had people around who loved me. But I guess I couldn't help but wonder what was wrong with me, you know? I always wondered if I'd been different—prettier, smarter, a better athlete—if my dad would've stuck around."

Nick traced his fingers along the back of her hand. Her hands were so soft and smooth. "He doesn't know what he missed. If he did, he'd spend his life trying to make it up to you."

Suzanne shrugged. "Maybe. Or maybe he just wasn't cut out to be a dad. I think that's been part of my problem. If my mom was that wrong when she chose a man to marry, then how in the world do I think I'll do any better?"

"So it's easier for you to not let yourself risk that kind of potential situation."

She nodded. "Exactly."

"And now?"

"I keep thinking back to that verse that's on my refrigerator. Sometimes I think maybe I'm too stubborn. I spend a lot of time trying to plan my life my way and never consider whether there's a bigger plan for me. I haven't done a great job of trusting that the Lord really has a plan for me. I say it, but there have been times I haven't believed it. I've felt like I was drifting aimlessly without realizing that maybe I wasn't drifting. Maybe I was actually headed in the direction I was supposed to go." She shrugged. "Does that seem crazy?"

"Not at all." He knew exactly where she was coming from. He'd spent a lot of time lately pondering God's plan for his own life, too. Sometimes it seemed so clear, and then other times. . .not so much. "I think the best thing to do is pray that the path for you will be clear. At least that's what I've started doing." He stood. "I doubt you got much sleep last night. I know I didn't. I'm going to get out of here and let you take a nap before you go see Charlie."

She rose and walked him to the door. "Thanks for coming over. And for being so honest about everything."

"It's the best policy." He grinned. "Even though it's not always the easiest."

Suzanne offered him a tiny smile. "I'll talk to you soon."

"Call me later and tell me how the little guy is doing, okay?"

She nodded.

He hesitated, then lightly brushed her lips with his. Although sharing his story with her had given him a sense of relief, he couldn't help but wish he'd kept it to himself. Because the closer he let her get, the harder it would be to leave. And with his grandmother's surgery at the end of the week, his departure was imminent.

fifteen

Nick paced the hallway at the hospital. It seemed like it had been a long time since his grandmother was wheeled into surgery. Aside from some distant cousins and a great aunt, she was the only family he had left in the world. He couldn't lose her. Even when he was in some far-off place, he never felt alone because he knew his grandmother was just a phone call away.

He'd tried to get Suzanne to prepare for the worst the other day about Charlie so she wouldn't have to deal with any more pain than necessary. But today he realized how important it was to have hope. Because otherwise, a time like this would be unbearable. He'd never understood how people who weren't believers got through times like these. He'd been praying almost nonstop, and it was such a comfort. But the people who dealt with a crisis like this and didn't rely on faith and didn't ask for prayers. . .how hopeless that must feel.

"Nick!"

He looked up to see Thomas St. Claire hurrying toward him. Grandmother had made sure Mr. St. Claire knew when her procedure was scheduled. She'd said it was for the extra prayers, but Nick suspected it comforted her to know he was there.

"Sorry I'm late. Traffic is terrible. Is Madelyn already in surgery?" His bushy gray eyebrows met above his nose.

Nick nodded and peered at his watch. "They took her back about thirty minutes ago." It seemed like three times that long.

"Was she upset that I wasn't here? Or did she even realize it?" Mr. St. Claire asked worriedly.

"I didn't get the chance to see her either. They were already prepping her when I got here." He smiled at the older man. "I'm sure she's fine."

Mr. St. Claire nodded. "I'll keep praying though, just in case." He sat down in one of the waiting room chairs and cupped his head in his hands.

"There you are," a voice called from down the corridor.

Nick looked up to see Suzanne hurrying toward him. "What are you doing here?" he asked once she'd made her way to him. He hadn't seen her since the day he told her the truth about his parents and brother. They'd spoken on the phone, but he'd come up with an excuse why he couldn't get together. After years of keeping people at a safe distance, he felt overwhelmed by their growing relationship.

She smiled. "Just here to offer my moral support. I took off a little early so I could be here for you." She sat down next to him.

He stiffened. It wasn't that he wasn't happy to see her, but he certainly didn't want to get accustomed to having her next to him in situations like this. He needed to deal with his grandmother's surgery on his own. "There's nothing to be done here but wait."

She reached over and clutched his arm. "I can wait with you."

He sighed. "You don't have to do that."

"I know I don't *have* to. But I thought you might want the company."

Nick managed a smile. "It could be hours. I'm fine by myself." He motioned toward Mr. St. Claire. "Mr. St. Claire is here in case I need anything."

Suzanne released his arm and stood. "Well then I guess you have everything under control." She turned to go, but not before he saw the hurt look in her blue eyes. "Call me sometime tomorrow and let me know how it went." Without another word she headed back the way she'd come.

Nick rose to go after her. *Just let her go, man.* He sat back down. Having Suzanne hold his hand while he waited for Grandmother's surgery to be over would only add to his ever-growing confusion. There had been times lately when he found himself seriously considering what a future with her would be like.

But he wasn't ready for that kind of commitment. So it was best to just let her go.

❧

Suzanne wished she hadn't acted impulsively. She almost never did anything like that. Just showing up out of the blue at the hospital like she was really his girlfriend or something. *What was I thinking?*

She dashed inside the house and quickly changed into her running clothes. She was already five minutes late to meet Emily. It seemed weird to go to Sea Isle Park without Charlie.

Once she got to the park, Emily waved her over. She stood next to her BMW, stretching her legs. "Hey, stranger. Sounds like you've had some kind of week."

Suzanne had given Emily the highlights and lowlights of the past few days when they spoke on the phone last night.

"Yeah. It's like I've been walking a tightrope lately."

"How's Charlie?" Emily asked as they started to walk briskly along the sidewalk.

Suzanne couldn't keep the grin off of her face. "I talked to the vet earlier. He's doing really well. I'll get to bring him home in a couple of days." Watching Charlie get hit by that car definitely ranked among the worst things that had ever happened to her.

"That's great." Emily glanced over at her. "I can't imagine how scary that was for you. I know how much you love that dog."

Suzanne nodded. "I had a huge epiphany though as I was waiting to find out if he made it through the night."

"Ooh. I love those," Emily said with a grin. "Spill it."

"I had this weird thought that if I didn't have Charlie—if I'd never gotten him from the pound—I wouldn't have to go through those emotions. Because I wouldn't have an attachment to him. You know?"

Emily nodded.

"But then I realized that having Charlie as my pet for the past ten years has given me more happiness than the pain that might come from losing him. And then I started thinking about the rest of my life and how I've been essentially staying away from a serious relationship because it might cause me pain. But what if the happiness from the relationship is bigger than any pain it could ever cause? Does that make sense to you? It's just something I'm considering."

Emily beamed. "It makes perfect sense to me. Kind of like that old adage, 'I'd rather to have loved and lost than never to have loved at all,' right?"

"Exactly," Suzanne said.

"What about the 5K? Was it awful?"

Suzanne laughed. “The best part was the doughnuts that were waiting at the end, if that tells you anything.” She grinned. “Actually it wasn’t too bad. But I’m thinking running in a half marathon in three months is a little ambitious.”

“So we should stick to the 5K instead?”

Suzanne nodded. “Probably best. I mean, Nick beat my time, and he hasn’t been training like I have. So I’m thinking I should probably hold off on an even longer distance until I know I’m ready. But if you run the half marathon, I will totally cheer you on.”

“I’m not exactly ready to run thirteen miles, and the way my schedule is, I don’t know that I will be ready by December.” Emily smiled. “But I’m glad you had someone to run with last weekend. How is Airplane Nick anyway?”

Suzanne frowned. “At this point, maybe we should use a nickname for him after all.”

“Did y’all finally have a bad date? Because I was starting to think he was some kind of Prince Charming with all of the doing and saying the right things he had going on.”

“Not a bad date. Just a bad case of stupidity.” She’d known going into this thing with Nick that his heart was off the table. Yet, she’d kept seeing him.

Emily stopped walking as they passed a park bench. “Let’s sit for a minute while you explain yourself.”

“Nick hasn’t made any effort to hide the fact that he’s out of here as soon as his grandmother recuperates. He’s never given me any indication that he might want a relationship with me.”

Emily snorted. “Except for kissing you and holding your hand and trying to spend as much time with you as possible. Just those little things, but who’s counting?”

Suzanne twisted her mouth into a smile. Her friends always had her back. Even when she didn't make smart choices, they were on her side. "Sure. His actions may have said one thing, but his words said another. And his words were very clear—he doesn't want any complications, and he is leaving as soon as he can."

"You fell for him, didn't you?" Emily asked quietly.

Suzanne didn't say anything for a long moment. "Do I have to answer that?"

"Nope. Because it's written all over your face."

"I went to the hospital to sit with him during his grandmother's surgery. I thought I would be a comfort to him, you know? When Charlie got hit by that car, Nick took us to the vet and sat with me in the waiting room. I was so thankful I wasn't going through it alone." She sighed. "I guess I just thought he'd want me there."

"And it didn't go that way?"

Suzanne shook her head. "Hardly. He wasn't rude or anything, but he definitely gave me the impression that I wasn't wanted." *Well, maybe he was borderline rude.*

"You think he was just worried?"

Suzanne stretched her legs out in front of her. "I tried to believe that at first, but pretty soon it became obvious. As soon as I walked in, he tensed up. Maybe it's just too much for him. I mean, you give me a hard time about being commitment-phobic, but Nick is way worse than me."

"If that's true, maybe you should just walk away. Because there's nothing worse than being with a guy who isn't capable of a real commitment." Emily had gone through a broken engagement last year after her longtime boyfriend decided he wasn't ready to settle down.

"I'm just trying to take it one day at a time. I mean, he'll probably be leaving soon anyway. I wish he'd decide to stay here and see where things between us could go, but I'm not holding out much hope for that." She sighed. "I do have a little piece of good news though."

"Yeah? What's that?"

"I'm meeting with a Realtor next week." She'd prayed about her housing situation ever since she learned that her rental house was going up for sale. And then the day before yesterday, while she was searching the local real estate sites for possible rentals, she'd stumbled upon the perfect house for sale. In her neighborhood. And in her price range.

Emily raised her eyebrows in surprise. "No way. You've put that off forever. I thought you didn't want anything to tie you down." Right after her breakup, Emily had purchased a condo in an historic building downtown. Her favorite hobby was home renovations, and she'd roped Suzanne into all kinds of do-it-yourself projects.

"I'll bet you're regretting that week you made me spend helping you to gut your guest bathroom, aren't you?" Suzanne laughed. "Because if I buy a house I'm going to expect payback." She grinned. "Seriously though, I guess I'm just finally at a point where putting down roots doesn't seem so scary. I'm kind of excited about the idea of my own place."

"It's a big step for you. I can't help but wonder if Airplane Nick doesn't have something to do with it."

Suzanne shrugged. "Maybe. But not in the way you think. Nick showed me that it's possible to care about someone but not lose myself. I've always been afraid of being one of those girls who just becomes a copy of whoever she dates. But Nick seems to appreciate me the way I am. Even if he doesn't appreciate me enough to stay here, I believe I'll meet someone who will."

sixteen

Nick helped his grandmother out of her wheelchair and into the waiting Lexus. He smiled at the nurse who'd wheeled her out. "Thanks for your help."

"Our pleasure." The woman smiled then leaned into the car to see his grandmother. "Now you take care of yourself, Miss Madelyn. We'll see you soon for your checkup, but in the meantime, try and follow the doctor's orders, okay?"

"You medical people act like I'm going to go run with the bulls or jump out of a plane," Grandmother said with a huff. "I promise to act like the old lady that I am, at least until Dr. Eubanks gives me the all clear." Her eyes twinkled. "And then all bets are off."

The nurse shook her head and glanced at Nick. "Watch this one, okay? She's feisty." She closed the passenger door and waved at Grandmother.

Nick nodded. "I will, and I know she is." He grinned. "Where do you think I got it?" He climbed into the driver's seat and glanced at his grandmother. "You ready to get home?"

She nodded. "I've been ready all morning. What took you so long to get here?"

He laughed. "Aren't you the woman who used to remind me that patience is a virtue?"

"Patience is a virtue. But being cooped up inside of a hospital waiting for your grandson to pick you up tends to make one a bit cranky." She looked over at him with a smile.

"Sorry I was a little late. I overslept and then hit traffic." Nick merged onto the interstate and headed toward Germantown.

"I hope you overslept because you stayed out too late with that nice girl, Suzanne. She seems like quite a catch."

Ever since he'd introduced them, Grandmother had been singing Suzanne's praises. "She's nice, but I didn't see her last night." Actually it had been a couple of days since he'd gone out with Suzanne. They'd had dinner a couple of days after Grandmother's surgery and finally gotten to go to Houston's and the drive-in. It had been fun, and Nick had even confessed to her about his sophomoric prank that got him banned from the outdoor theater for the rest of his high school career. She'd threatened to tell the manager and see if Nick's name was still on some kind of banned list. They ate popcorn and held hands, and at the end of the night he'd come really close to telling her that he had strong feelings for her. But he stopped himself in time. Just because he cared about her didn't change things.

Settling down wasn't part of his plans.

"Have you given any thought to what we discussed the other day?" Grandmother asked.

He sighed. "Staying in Memphis isn't an option. I'm really sorry." He offered a grin in the hopes it would placate her, but judging by her expression, his charm hadn't worked. "But I'll visit more often, I promise."

"Nicholas, please consider what you're giving up. You're at the age where it's time to think about starting a life with someone. Don't you want to have children of your own someday?"

He shrugged. "My life is fine the way it is. And I'm not sure about children. Maybe I should get a pet first." He chuckled.

Grandmother didn't look amused. "I'm not going to be around forever. And I know you'd like to believe that you don't need anyone, but take it from my years of experience—life is better when it's shared."

He didn't say anything as he pulled the car down the long driveway. "Maybe someday I'll get to that place. But I'm not there yet." He shifted the car into PARK and killed the engine.

Grandmother stared at him with sad eyes. "Think about what your parents would want for you, dear. Do you think they'd want you to spend holidays on some cruise ship in the Mediterranean trying to pretend they never existed?"

He frowned. "I don't pretend they never existed. I just try not to remember that chapter of my life." He slid out of the car and walked around to help her out. He loved his grandmother dearly, but her butting into his life wasn't helping her cause any.

Besides, last night when he couldn't sleep he'd made a decision that could be the answer to all his problems. He'd just have to see if Suzanne was on board.

❧

Suzanne paced the length of her living room until she feared she'd worn a groove in the floor. Nick had called an hour ago and let her know he was coming over.

Because they needed to talk.

Suzanne was quite sure that nowhere in the history of the universe had a conversation that followed the words "we need to talk" ever been successful. She didn't even want to guess what Nick so urgently needed to talk to her about.

Except that one tiny, niggling thought wouldn't leave her

alone. Maybe he wanted to tell her that he cared about her. That he had feelings, real feelings for her. The kind of feelings that made him want to abandon his vagabond lifestyle and stay here so they could see where things between them might go.

Don't be stupid. Suzanne hated to even let herself consider that something like that could be the motivation for his visit. He probably wanted to get her opinion on what city he should move to next or brainstorm an article he was writing or have her help him order flowers for his grandmother. It probably didn't have anything to do with the murky relationship they'd struck up this summer.

The doorbell rang and she froze. She glanced down at her outfit. She hadn't changed after work because the slim black skirt and white button-down shirt always garnered compliments. A wide black belt emphasized her waist, and her red heels gave the outfit a pop of color. It was one of those outfits that always gave her confidence, and considering what might face her on the other side of the door, she needed it.

She flung the door open. "Hi."

Nick's appreciative gaze told her she'd chosen her clothing wisely. "Thanks for seeing me. I know it was short notice." He grinned and walked inside.

Charlie raised his head from the couch but didn't get up.

Nick went to him. "Hey, buddy. I'm glad you're okay," he said softly. He gently scratched the dog behind the ear.

"It's good to have him home. The place was way too quiet and lonely without him." She motioned toward the recliner. "Have a seat."

Nick sat stiffly on the leather recliner. "You look nice today," he said.

She perched on the couch next to Charlie. "Thank you." She jerked her chin toward the kitchen. "Do you want something to drink?"

He shook his head. "No thanks."

"How's your grandmother?"

He grinned. "Three days home and she's ordering everyone around like a general. A couple of her friends from church have been helping me take care of her, and she's keeping us hopping. I honestly think that woman could run the country if given the chance. But she's feeling great. Her follow-up appointment went well."

Suzanne nodded. "That's wonderful news. I'm so glad to hear that she's okay."

"Which is kind of what I wanted to talk to you about. . . ." Nick trailed off and locked eyes with her. "Look, Suzanne, there's no denying that there's something between us."

This is it. He's finally going to tell me how he feels. She nodded. "Right."

"I'm so incredibly thankful that I met you on the plane." He smiled. "Because you've made the past few weeks so much easier than I expected them to be." He raked his fingers through his hair. "And I'd really like to stay in touch after I leave."

Her stomach tightened. "Stay in touch?" *It sounds like he wants to be my pen pal or something. Not exactly the declaration I was hoping for.*

Nick chuckled. "I know you're like the queen of long-distance relationships. So if you're up for some cross-country trips, I was kind of hoping maybe we could keep seeing each other." He smiled like he'd just offered her the moon.

"Long distance?" She should've known.

"I'm still deciding where to move next. I'm heading to New York for a little while, at least through the holidays." He grinned. "So many people visit there at Christmastime, I figure it'll be impossible to be lonely." He widened his eyes. "Hey, maybe you could come for a visit sometime in December. We could ice skate at Rockefeller Center and go to FAO Schwartz. Wouldn't that be fun?"

She frowned.

"That face doesn't say 'Christmas in New York sounds fun,' so what gives?" He leaned forward and rubbed her bare knee. "If you prefer someplace warmer we could meet in Florida. Maybe Disney or something." He looked at her expectantly.

Suzanne worked hard to keep her jaw from dropping. "You're serious?"

"Sure am." He grinned. "Maybe Florida is the way to go. Who wouldn't want a suntan in winter?"

She rose from her spot on the couch, her mind reeling. "I'm going to get some water. You sure you don't want something?"

He narrowed his eyes and shook his head. "No thanks. I'll just hang out here with Charlie."

Suzanne hurried out of the living room and into the kitchen. She grabbed a bottle of water out of the refrigerator and took a tiny sip. Her eyes fell on the dry-erase board that was stuck to the refrigerator. She still hadn't moved past the verse from Jeremiah. She'd spent the past few months praying that she'd figure out God's plan for her life. That it would be clear.

The only thing clear to her right this minute was that she had no interest in another long-distance relationship with anyone.

Not even Nick.

She squared her shoulders and strode back into the living room. "I appreciate what you're saying here," she said. "And I have no doubt that you and I would have a wonderful time in New York or Florida or wherever we met up." She managed a tiny smile. "But I think I'm done with the long-distance phase of my life."

He frowned. "I don't understand. I thought you and I wanted the same thing. I thought you didn't have any interest in settling down and all that it entails."

Suzanne took her place on the couch and absently stroked Charlie's soft fur. "That used to be true. It's not any longer." She shook her head. "You want to know the irony of this situation? It's your fault that long distance isn't enough for me anymore."

"My fault? How so?"

"It's been so nice having you around. Grabbing dinner after work. Running with me in the 5K. Having you on the other end of the phone at the end of the day or sending me funny texts while I'm at work. All those things have been real eye-openers. And on the day Charlie got hit—even though you and I weren't on the same page part of the time—having you to lean on while I was going through a tough time really made me stop and think. For the first time, I started to see that a future with someone doesn't have to be the prison I've always been afraid it would be. Instead, I realized that having a partner in life could be amazing. If it was the right partner, I mean." She'd really thought that person could be him. But it looked like he didn't feel the same.

"So maybe we should just try this for a little while. See

where it goes?" He looked at her hopefully.

She shook her head. "I'm certain that a long-distance relationship isn't enough for me any longer." Unexpected tears sprang into her eyes. Letting go of Nick would be so hard. But she needed more stability than he could offer. And even though she would probably always be cautious as a result of her parents' divorce, she believed that she could find a happily ever after of her own. And that didn't include a part-time boyfriend.

Nick bit his bottom lip. "I didn't see this coming. I don't know what to say."

"You could say that you're staying." She met his gaze. "You could say that you want to stay here and fight for me. . .for us. You could say that you want me to be part of your life bad enough that you're willing to make some compromises."

He lowered his head. "I wish I could say those things. But you know I can't."

Suzanne nodded. She'd expected as much, but that didn't stop it from hurting. "You kissed me like you could though." Some things couldn't be undone. She'd known better than to give her heart to a drifter, and she'd gone and done it anyway. The only bright spot in the situation as far as she could see was that at least she knew now that it was possible for her to have real feelings for someone. It was possible for her to care enough about someone that she could actually be open to settling down. In her world, that was huge.

"I'm not going to apologize for kissing you. My leaving now doesn't diminish anything between us. I hope you know that."

Suzanne let out a breath. "When do you leave?"

"I'm booked on a flight out on Sunday." He cleared his

throat. "I guess there's no point in asking you to go out with me one last time, huh?"

She shook her head. "I don't think that's a good idea. One more dinner isn't going to make saying good-bye to you any easier." She sighed. "Nick, I hope you find whatever it is that you're searching for. I hoped it might be me, but I can see in your eyes that you aren't sure about that. And I'm looking for someone who is sure about me. Someone who is willing to take a risk for me. There's a teeny-tiny part of me that hopes someday you'll look back on this moment with regret. Sorry about that." She managed a tiny smile. "I guess when it boils down to it, I'm just like any other girl. I want the fairy tale."

Nick closed his eyes and shook his head slowly. "You're not like any other girl. I hope you know that." He stood. "I guess this is good-bye then."

She walked him to the door.

He reached out and pulled her into an embrace.

Suzanne rested her head on his shoulder and let herself relax in his arms.

Nick brushed his lips against her forehead. "I'll miss you," he whispered softly. "If you change your mind, you have my number."

She nodded. "Likewise."

Nick let go of her, and she watched him walk slowly down the driveway. She watched out the window until she couldn't see his car anymore.

Then she curled up on the couch next to Charlie and stopped trying to hold back the tears. *Lord, I know You have a plan for me. Please show me what it is, and take this hurt away as soon as possible.*

seventeen

Nick had been in New York for a week and had barely left his hotel room. He'd met Richard for dinner one night, but that was about it.

He picked up his cell phone then put it back down. He'd done that a lot the past few days. He hadn't realized how much he and Suzanne had kept in contact by texting and calling until he'd told her good-bye and the texting stopped.

He opened the curtains and stared out into the city. There'd been a time not too long ago when looking out over a city skyline would've thrilled him to no end. But tonight all he could think of was how much he wished Suzanne were there to share it with him.

You're seriously losing it, man. He grabbed his fleece jacket and strode out of the hotel. Late September in New York was beautiful, but he couldn't help but wonder what it was like in Memphis. It had been a lot of years, but he could still remember those first delicious days of fall when the hot air that had blanketed the city all summer finally started to cool down. His dad had always called it football weather. Warm during the day and just cool enough at night to require a light jacket.

Nick wandered aimlessly down Broadway, passing couples walking hand in hand. All these years and it had never bothered him to see other people's happiness because he was content with his life just the way it was. There was always someone to go to dinner with or catch a movie with, and that was all he required. Those casual dates had always been enough for him in the past, but when Richard had mentioned a woman he wanted to fix him up with, Nick had declined. Made an excuse about needing to focus on his writing. A date with a random girl suddenly seemed very empty.

He turned off the main drag and groaned out loud as he saw the marquee for the theater he was in front of. *Memphis, the Musical.*

Suzanne had seen it when the traveling show came to the Orpheum, and she'd said it was amazing. Nick figured the Broadway production would be even better. He glanced at his watch and hurried to the box office. He might be in New York, but for the next couple of hours he could visit Memphis.

❧

Suzanne signed her name on the contract with a flourish.

"Congratulations, Miss Simpson, you're officially a homeowner." The closing agent held out a key ring with two keys. "I hope you enjoy your first home very much. It's been a pleasure working with you."

Suzanne clutched the keys and stared at them. She'd always expected that she'd get to this moment and be nauseated and feel like she'd signed her life away. Instead she was completely certain of the decision. *I'm a homeowner.*

She thanked the Realtor and closing agent and walked outside to her SUV. She drove over to the rental house to finish packing. The leaves were just beginning to change in her neighborhood, adding a splash of orange to the green that was so prevalent during the summer. She looked forward to crisp fall days and already planned to plant brightly colored mums at her new home. *My new home.* It hadn't sunk in yet.

Her phone buzzed. "Hello," she said, pulling into the driveway.

"Well? Is everything done?" Emily asked excitedly.

She laughed. Her friends were almost as excited about her place as she was. Emily and Jade had both promised to help her paint, and Jade had arranged for some of the members of their care group from church to lend a hand on moving day. "Everything is done now except for the hard part. You know, the actual moving. And the painting. And the decorating."

"Oh, that's the fun part. You'll have tons of help, so don't worry."

Suzanne grinned as she opened the back door and let Charlie out into the fenced yard. He'd healed nicely. His progress pleased the vet, especially considering the dog's advanced age. "I know I have help. And believe me, I'm totally appreciative."

"Is there anything else you need to tell me? I'm about to go into the hospital."

"I don't guess so," she said innocently. "Why?"

Emily groaned. "You are impossible. I know good and well you are sitting on two pieces of news. Stop holding out."

Suzanne laughed. "Okay, okay. I decided to interview for that job at Youth Villages that Jade's friend told me about." She'd finally decided to break out of her work rut.

"Awesome. What kind of position is it?"

"Community relations. I think it sounds perfect. A little bit of event planning, a little bit of community outreach, and there's a social media component. It sounds like exactly what I've been hoping to find." Suzanne had felt hesitant at first, but she'd resolved to take the opportunities that came her way and stop letting fear hold her back. So when Jade's friend mentioned the opening, she sent in her résumé right away. Her interview was coming up next week.

"That sounds amazing. Let me know as soon as you find out if you get it."

Suzanne smiled. "I will."

"And did James e-mail you yet? I've been dying to know, but I didn't want to ask him or else he might think I'm some kind of crazy matchmaker." Dr. James Addington was Emily's colleague at St. Jude. Emily had been trying for months to get Suzanne to agree to at least let her arrange an e-mail introduction.

Suzanne had stood her ground against the setup for a long time but had finally agreed that it might not be a bad idea to at least meet James. "We've exchanged two e-mails since you did your little introduction. He seems very nice, just busy."

"Busy's good. That means he's gainfully employed." Emily chuckled. "Seriously, he's a nice guy. I'd go out with him myself except that I really don't want to date someone from work." Emily had very specific rules for herself that she always followed.

"I'm not sure if we'll get together or not, but at least it's nice to have a prospect. He got my phone number yesterday, so I think he's supposed to call soon."

Emily squealed. "Perfect. You'll have to text me if he does."

"I will. And if I meet him, he'd better be as normal as you say he is. The last time I let someone set me up I ended up on a date with a guy who loved birds. He talked about birds all night, and when I found out a three-foot bird lives in his house, I thanked him for the coffee and left."

Emily burst out laughing. "I'd forgotten about Crazy Bird Man. Jade set you up with that one, right?"

"Yep. Never again."

"Well for what it's worth, I'm really proud of you for all the stuff you're doing. I know change isn't easy for you, and yet here you are—a new house, a potential new job, and a new guy."

"Thanks. I guess I finally decided my life wasn't turning out exactly the way I wanted it to, and it was time to make some changes."

"Well I was afraid you'd let the thing with Airplane Nick impact your life. I'm glad to see that you're moving on. I have to run now; I'm at the hospital. I'll talk to you soon."

They said their good-byes, and Suzanne sank into one of the chairs on her patio. The holidays were coming up before too long. Her goal was to have her new house ready for entertaining by mid-November. She'd love to host a holiday party or something.

She opened the kitchen door and herded Charlie through. The house was in shambles. There were boxes everywhere along with an ever-growing pile of items to send to Goodwill. She sighed. May as well get back to work.

She didn't mind staying busy because it kept her mind off things. Even though she'd moved on with her life instead of sitting around wishing things with Nick had turned out differently, she still wondered how he was doing and if she'd ever hear from him again.

She was moving forward as best as she could, but Nick still had a little piece of her heart.

Wherever in the world he was.

eighteen

Nick grabbed his suitcase from the baggage carousel and headed through the double doors. It was hard to believe he'd been away from Memphis for nearly two months. What if he was making a terrible mistake? He'd never been one to second-guess himself, but ever since he said good-bye to Suzanne he'd been doing just that.

He walked outside and caught sight of his grandmother's gold Lexus. He grinned broadly and hurried to her car. He opened the back door and slid his bag inside. "Hi there," he said to his grandmother. "Do you want me to drive?"

She pressed her lips together and shook her head. "I've been driving myself around for more years than you've been alive, thank you very much." She beamed as he settled into the passenger seat. "I'm so glad you're here. And I hope you're going to stay through the holidays."

Nick had a reason for being here besides just checking up on Grandmother's health, but he didn't want to tell her his plans. He'd always been the kind of guy who only took very calculated risks—the kind he was certain would have the outcome he desired. Yet here he was, setting out on a mission that could be an epic failure. "I'm not sure about my plans just yet, but I'm glad to be here now."

Grandmother smiled. "Are you going to see that nice Suzanne while you're in town? I hope you will. You should invite her over for dinner one night."

Nick sighed. It was time to steer the subject away from himself. "What did the doctor say last week? Is everything okay?"

"Oh yes. I'm doing very well. I'm already looking forward to planting my spring flowers."

"I'm glad to hear it."

Grandmother slowed the car down as they reached her street. She pulled into the driveway and glanced over at Nick. "Are you coming inside now, or do you need to borrow the car?" She raised an eyebrow.

"I'd like to borrow the car for a bit if that's okay." He grinned.

She nodded. "I figured." She climbed out of the car and waited on him at the front of the vehicle.

Nick wrapped his grandmother in a big hug. "Thanks for letting me take the car. I'll be back in time for dinner. If you need me to pick anything up, just call." He kissed her on the cheek.

"Tell Suzanne I said hello," she called over her shoulder as she walked up the porch steps.

He groaned and eased into the car. The woman could read him like a book. And here he thought he'd been so sneaky, flying into town under the guise of checking on her. He started the car and drove over to Suzanne's house. He just hoped she was home. Some Saturdays she had to work. But if she wasn't home, he could wait.

He pulled into the driveway, and an unfamiliar Jeep Liberty sat in her normal parking space. She hadn't told him she was getting a new vehicle, but then he hadn't talked to her in a couple of months. It was a sweet ride though.

Nick couldn't keep the smile from his face. He knocked on the door and waited, listening for Charlie's familiar bark.

A man he'd never seen opened the door halfway. "Can I help you?" he asked, a suspicious look on his face.

Nick bit his lip. He hadn't considered that she could have a boyfriend. *What an idiot. She's moved on, and I've been holding on to a memory.* "I'm looking for Suzanne Simpson."

The man furrowed his brow. "You've got the wrong house." He started to shut the door, but Nick grabbed it.

"I know she lived here two months ago."

The man shrugged. "And I moved in last month."

Nick walked back to the car in defeat. So much for the element of surprise. He'd have to call her. He pulled out his phone and scrolled through his contacts until he found her name. He touched the screen, and her picture popped up. She'd been laughing at something he'd said when he snapped it. What a dummy he'd been. He touched the screen again and listened to the rings. "Hello," an unfamiliar voice said on the other end.

"I–I'm afraid I must have a bad connection. I was trying to call Suzanne Simpson."

The woman on the other end laughed. "Suzanne doesn't work here anymore, so she had to turn her phone in. And since it was newer than mine, I inherited it." She laughed again. "I'm Avis, and if you need some assistance with a Graceland wedding, I'm your girl."

Suzanne had mentioned Avis a couple of times. "Suzanne doesn't work there anymore?" he asked. Had she left town? Gone back to Mississippi?

"No."

"Where does she work? And where is she living now?"

"Look, buddy, I'm sure you're all kinds of nice, but for all I know you could be a total creep. So I don't think it's a good idea for me to give out Suzanne's personal information."

Nick sighed. "Please. I flew in from New York to see her. I went to her house, and she doesn't live there anymore, and now I call her cell phone and find out she doesn't work at Graceland anymore. I can try to search the city, but it would be much easier if you'd just help me."

Avis clucked her tongue. "Do I have the pleasure of speaking to Nick? It must be my lucky day. I've heard a lot about you."

He breathed a sigh of relief. If she'd heard Suzanne talk about him, then surely she'd help him out. "I've heard about you, too. And I hope you'll help me."

Avis grew quiet for a long moment. "Well, Nick, do you think she'll be happy to see you or not? Because I don't want to cause her any trouble."

"I think she'll be happy to see me. I know I'll be happy to see her. And I'd really like to surprise her by showing up out of the blue." He grinned at the thought. "I'm hoping she'll think it's kind of romantic."

"Aww, that's sweet," Avis said with a laugh. "Normally I'd just take your name and number and pass the information along to her, but I heard all about you over the summer. I think you were good for her. So I'll play along with your surprise. You got a pen? I'll give you her new address. It's in the same neighborhood as her old place."

He scribbled down the address. It looked to be just a few blocks over from her rental. "Thanks Avis; you're a peach."

She giggled. "Good luck."

He ended the call and stared at the address. It was now or never.

Five minutes later he pulled into Suzanne's new driveway. He walked up the steps to the front porch. Two large terra cotta pots filled with mums lined each side of the door. He rang the doorbell and waited.

The pounding in his chest quickened as he heard the lock turn on the other side of the door. The door swung open, and he was right where he'd dreamed of being for the past few weeks.

Face-to-face with Suzanne.

❧

Suzanne felt as if the wind had been knocked out of her. She'd been expecting the delivery guy from Ashley Furniture. Today was the day she was finally getting her new brown leather couch. But that definitely wasn't a couch on her porch. "What are you doing here?" she asked.

He grinned. "That's all you can say? Do you have any idea how much trouble it was to track you down?"

She waved him inside. "I can imagine." *If you'd have called me after you left, you would've known I moved.*

He hesitated for a moment before giving her a quick hug. "So a new house and a new job? You've been really busy since I left."

She fought to keep her face neutral. Hugging Nick and breathing in his familiar smell made her want to throw caution to the wind and see if his long-distance offer was still on the table. But she couldn't do that. She deserved more. "I think I told you that my lease was up and they were selling the place. Well, I decided I was ready to buy." She gestured around the living room. "What do you think?"

Nick glanced around and nodded. "It's nice. I'm happy for you." He grinned.

"Thanks. I moved in about a month ago, and it's been really fun to fix it up the way I want. There's still some painting to do, and eventually I'd like to put down laminate flooring, but I really like it so far." She smiled. "And Charlie loves the backyard. It's way better than the rental."

He raked his fingers through his hair. It was much shorter than it had been when they met. He looked like a real grown-up now and not someone clinging to his frat boy days.

"So why are you in town anyway? I didn't know if I'd ever see you again." After a few weeks, she'd come to terms with the idea of never seeing Nick again. She hadn't been happy about it but figured it might be for the best. In hindsight, she definitely felt like she'd cared more for him than he had for her. That was a tough pill to swallow, but she had to trust that God had someone even better in store for her—someone who wouldn't be afraid of his feelings.

He sighed. "I came to see you. I made a huge mistake before. I spent the past two months trying to get back into the swing of writing and traveling, but my mind kept drifting to you."

"Why didn't you call?" She'd spent the first three weeks after he left with her phone practically glued to her. But his call never came. And then she'd turned her phone in at work and figured that was it. It was time to move on.

Nick shrugged. "I hoped an in-person visit would be more effective. I knew I needed to see you face-to-face."

"So what exactly do you mean when you say you made a mistake?"

"I'm trying to change my ways. I'm thinking of putting down roots somewhere." He shrugged. "And I just hoped that would be enough for you to consider continuing to see me."

Suzanne sighed. "Nick, I care a lot about you. And I wish I could give you the answer you want. But I'm doing my thing here. It isn't easy, but I'm doing it. I bought the house, and I started a new job a couple of weeks ago. It's a lot of change in a very short time."

"And I think what you've done is wonderful. I know what a big step all of that was for you."

"Right. I told you once that I wasn't going to let my fear of the unknown hold me back any longer, and I meant it. . .except where my personal life is concerned."

He furrowed his brow. "What do you mean?"

"I know that you're saying you want to change and you want to find a more permanent life and all, but from where I sit it would be very hard for me to trust that you can go through with it." She wished she could believe him. And it wasn't that she thought he was lying per se, but she just didn't think he was really ready to change.

"I don't understand. I thought you wanted to hear me say that I was going to settle down. And that's what I'm saying."

"But you haven't actually done it yet, have you? When did you even get here?"

He coughed. "A couple of hours ago."

"So this is really just a plan, right? If I agree, then you're going to settle down and put down roots, but if I don't agree, you're gone again? Off to who knows where?"

Nick scratched his chin. "Pretty much."

She wanted to say yes. But it just didn't feel right. "I can't be the reason." She shook her head. "Because then if this doesn't work out and you've put down roots and settled down just because you think that's what I want, you are going to resent me. If you're ready to have a home—a real home—with a job that doesn't have you flying around the world at a moment's notice and stable friends and all that goes along with it, that's great. But the fact that you're here without any of that leads me to wonder if you're really serious."

Nick's jaw tensed. "Suzanne, you know that I. . ." He grew silent.

You what? Love me? If only he could say those words she might be able to believe that he'd changed his ways. But from what she could tell, this visit wasn't very well thought out. He was the same Nick he'd been two months ago when he'd made it clear that all he was capable of was a long-distance relationship.

"Never mind," Nick said finally. "I shouldn't have come. I wanted to see you though." He sighed. "I really have missed you."

But not enough to call. Not enough to keep in touch. Not enough to definitively say the words she'd hoped to hear. "I've missed you, too. I hope you'll let me know if you come into town again." She smiled to try to take some of the tension out of the situation. "But next time a little notice might be good."

He nodded. "I'm happy for you. The new house and the new job. . . It looks like you're really on a good path."

Suzanne managed a tiny smile. "Thanks." She walked him to the door, once again wondering if she'd ever see him again.

Nick waved and headed outside to the car.

Suzanne shut the door behind her and considered what he'd said. Could he be serious about wanting to change? Only time would tell. But she wouldn't hold her breath. Since they met, Nick had regaled her with one tale after another about his travels and adventures. He wouldn't give up that freedom easily.

nineteen

Nick paced the length of his old bedroom. All summer he'd stayed at his grandmother's and managed not to step foot in here. But when he'd gotten back from Suzanne's yesterday, Grandmother had ushered him up the stairs.

"I put clean sheets on your old bed," she'd said. "While you're here, I hope you can go through some of the things in the attic and in your closet."

When the St. Claires bought Nick's parents' home, most of the belongings had been moved to Grandmother's attic. Nick hadn't even gone up there during the two years he lived in her house while he finished high school. Maybe it was finally time to face it. It had been twelve years after all. Besides, it shouldn't be his grandmother's responsibility. She might give off an air of toughness, but losing her family had taken a huge toll on her.

Nick sat on the bed and picked up a framed picture from the nightstand. It was the last portrait his family had ever had made. They'd gone to Destin, Florida, for a week at the end of July every year for as long as he could remember. It seemed like half of Memphis went to Destin on vacation because they always ran into people they knew from school. That last summer, Nick had begged his parents to let him drive his own car, but his dad wouldn't hear of it. "You boys are getting older and are always running in different directions. For this one week, we're going to spend time as a family." They'd had such a wonderful time, tossing the football on the beach and eating seafood until they were stuffed. Nick's dad had given his mom a gift certificate to a spa, and she'd spent a day getting pampered. They'd come back home sun-kissed and rested and as close as ever. And in less than two months, everything had changed.

Nick slowly climbed up the stairs to the attic. Boxes and furniture filled the large space. He rifled through the first box he came to. Austin's stuff. His little brother would have been twenty-six now. Maybe he'd have married young like Ryan did and already have a kid or two. Austin had looked up to Nick so much, and Nick had always tried to set a good example. *What would you think of me now, little brother?*

Nick opened a large box and pulled out his dad's old letterman jacket. Nick used to wear it when he was in junior high and dream of the day he'd have one of his own. His dad had been so proud of him for his football skills. But he'd been even prouder the day Nick had become a Christian. Nick could still see Dad's broad smile and his tear-filled eyes. He'd hugged him and told him he was proud and that someday he hoped he'd get to see Nick's kids have their own relationship with Jesus.

Nick sat down in an antique-looking rocker. It had been the one his mother had used to rock him and Austin. She had such high hopes for her boys from day one. She'd taught them both to read before kindergarten and always made sure to talk to them about things going on in the world. He and his mom had discussed everything from politics to relationships when he was a teenager. "Find a woman who loves the Lord as much as you do and who wants to serve Him," she'd said once when Nick came home grumbling about girls. "Keeping the Lord in the center of your relationship is the key to a good marriage."

A good marriage. Nick had spent the past few years doubting he'd ever get married or have kids of his own. But lately he'd been wondering if there was more to life than travel and adventure. His time in New York had seemed empty. And he was pretty sure he knew why. Suzanne had gotten under his skin in a way no woman ever had. His family would've loved her if they'd gotten to meet her. He had no doubt about that.

A tap at the door made him jump.

Grandmother smiled from the doorway. "I'm glad you're looking through these things. I've sat up here many times over the years just to feel close to them." She shuffled through one of the boxes.

"I'm sorry," he said quietly.

Grandmother looked at him with confusion written all over her face. "Whatever for?"

"Leaving you here alone. Never coming to visit." His voice broke. "Trying to pretend that none of this happened."

She walked over to him and clasped his shoulder. "Nicholas, I never held that against you. I was always happy that you were off living your life, and I've prayed for ten years that you'd somehow find peace with the past."

Nick nodded. "I'm finally getting there, I think."

"They'd want you to live a full life, you know. One full of family and friends. You don't have to be alone."

He stood and hugged his grandmother. "Does that mean you'll let me stay here for the holidays?" he asked with a grin.

"I'd like nothing more." She returned his smile. "Now what do you say we go eat at Huey's? If you can make a toothpick stick in the ceiling, I'll buy your dinner." She winked and walked toward the door. "You coming?"

He nodded. "I'll be down in just a minute." Once she was gone, he pulled out his cell phone. "Ryan?" he said once his friend picked up. "You're not going to believe what I'm about to tell you, but I hope you'll agree to help an old friend out."

❧

Suzanne glanced around the table at her friends and grinned. "Thanks for coming y'all. I know this is a crazy time of year for everyone." She'd cooked a traditional Thanksgiving dinner for them the Sunday after Thanksgiving. She'd gone to Mississippi to see her family, but had made it back to Memphis that morning in time for church and spent the rest of the day breaking in her new kitchen.

"Don't be silly," Jade said. "It might be a busy time for normal people, but not for us. I mean, Emily has probably had her holiday shopping done since last July, and you know I haven't even started yet."

Emily laughed. "Not true. I still have one gift to buy. I never know what to get my boss." She narrowed her eyes at Jade. "But have you seriously not started shopping yet? It's already almost December. You totally stress me out."

Jade shrugged. "At first I thought I was going to make gifts. You know I've been doing a lot of painting lately, and I thought that could be a nice, personal gift. But I sort of ran out of time. And then I thought maybe I'd do something that mattered like make donations in people's names to their favorite charities or have trees planted or something." She dramatically put her head in her hands. "But that didn't seem personal enough."

"So you've been putting off the actual shopping, right?" Suzanne asked.

"Yep."

Emily grinned. "It's like I always say. . . Jade puts the 'pro' in procrastinator."

"Whatever. It'll get done." Jade sipped her sweet tea. "So Suzanne, if you need a shopping partner, call me. I mean, I'm sure you're not totally done like Miss Overachiever here." She grinned. "But you're probably further along than me."

"That sounds great. Maybe next week we can go to the mall out in Collierville." The outdoor mall was the newest one in town and one of Suzanne's favorite shopping spots.

"I want to hear what happened with James," Emily said. "I really had high hopes for that one."

Suzanne sat down at the head of her brand-new dining table. "I just wasn't quite ready. He's a very nice guy though." She raised an eyebrow in Jade's direction. "You want his e-mail?"

Jade shook her head. "No thanks. I'm on a dating sabbatical." She laughed. "I made the mistake of going out with that teacher again, and this time he took me to the worst restaurant I've ever been to. It was a buffet, and I promise you the only thing edible were the croutons on the salad bar. We each filled up a bowl with croutons, and that was our dinner. I thought for sure he'd at least offer to drive through McDonald's or something after that, but he didn't." She shook her head. "It's like I'm cursed."

"More like you should stop giving losers like that second

chances." Suzanne smiled. "Although it does make for some entertaining stories."

Emily patted the table to get their attention. "I'm sorry you had another bum date, Jade, but I'm with Suzanne. Our get-togethers wouldn't be the same if you didn't have a bad date story to tell." She turned to Suzanne with gleaming eyes. "Back to you and my doctor friend. Why do you think you aren't ready?" she pressed.

Suzanne propped her chin up on her hand and tried to figure out how to explain the situation without sounding like a complete basket case. "I don't think I'm quite over Nick yet."

"Seriously?" Emily let out a breath. "That guy is no good for you. I mean, he comes into town and acts like he's crazy about you and then wants a long-distance thing." She shook her head. "Airplane Nick wants to have his cake and eat it, too. Or whatever the saying is."

Suzanne nodded. "I know. If I really thought he wanted a normal, stable relationship, I would've said yes. But from everything I've seen of him, he just wants his freedom."

"Sounds a lot like someone else we know." Jade directed her gaze at Suzanne. "And you've changed. So why can't he?"

"I'm not saying he can't change. I'm saying that I don't think he wants to. Not really. If he'd cared about me enough, he never would've left Memphis in the first place, right? It's not like he had anywhere to go. He can do his job anywhere. So as far as I'm concerned, he chose freedom over me. It's that simple." Except that it wasn't that simple. Because as much as Suzanne had tried to forget Nick, she hadn't been able to so far.

"But you're happy, right?" Emily pressed.

Suzanne nodded. "I've never been happier with certain aspects of my life. I started praying with a purpose a few months ago. I've always prayed, but I guess in the past my prayers were sort of vague. Lately, I've started being really specific. I think that's helped me a lot. I started a prayer journal, and it's been really neat to be able to look back and actually see answered prayers." She shrugged. "Of course, sometimes the answer isn't what I'd hoped, but every time it ends up being exactly what I needed." She grinned. "Buying the house and starting the new job were both things I prayed about many times. And in each case, the path I was supposed to take became crystal clear."

"That's awesome," Jade said. "I know you've really struggled over the past months, especially since your grandpa died. I'm glad to know that you're in a good place."

Suzanne nodded. She *was* in a good place. For once in her life, she wasn't afraid of what the future may or may not hold. A tiny part of her still missed Nick, but she knew that eventually she'd move on.

And when she met the right guy, she'd be ready for a commitment. There'd been a time when the thought of marriage and kids made her want to hyperventilate. Even planning weddings at Graceland had been a challenge sometimes because when the bridal march would play, she'd start to get queasy.

But now the thought of commitment didn't scare her. Nick had shown her that there were guys out there she was compatible with. She needed to be patient. Just as she'd seen with the house and with the job, God had perfect timing. If the house had come along even a year ago, Suzanne wouldn't have been ready for home ownership. And if the job had come open six months ago, she wouldn't have applied. But the timing for each of those decisions had been right.

She knew without a shadow of a doubt that when the time came for her to meet the right man, she would. She just had to trust that God's plan for her life was better than her plan for her life. And so far, that had been true in spades.

Suzanne would keep praying and keep living her life. And if getting married and having a family was part of God's plan for her, she'd do it. And if not, she'd still have a wonderful and full life serving Him and doing whatever He called her to do next.

That thought was comforting and freeing at the same time.

twenty

Nick sat in the parking lot at Sea Isle Park and waited for Suzanne to show up. He had to admit, he felt a little like a stalker doing this. But he didn't see any other way. He had to make his case and hoped the element of surprise would work in his favor.

He took a deep breath. This was as close to standing out on a shaky ledge as he'd ever been.

Suzanne's Pathfinder pulled into a space a couple of rows over from him. She climbed out of the vehicle and helped Charlie jump out of the back end. Her hair was longer than it had been when they met, long enough to make a ponytail. She and Charlie set out toward the sidewalk.

This is it. He slid out of the truck and hurried toward her. "Suzanne," he called.

She whipped around. Her blue eyes widened as she recognized him. "Nick. What are you doing here?"

He grinned and jogged the rest of the way to her. "I needed to see you."

"A phone call would've been cheaper than the plane ticket here." She eyed him suspiciously. "Is your grandmother okay?"

Nick nodded. "She says she feels sixty again. And she's finally admitted that Mr. St. Claire is her 'man friend,' as she calls him." He grinned. "But I didn't come to town because of her. I came to see you."

She didn't say anything. Her face remained a neutral mask. Had she taken lessons in poker face over the past weeks?

He drew a breath and tried to remember all the things he'd rehearsed. "I've had time to do a lot of thinking over the past weeks about what's really important. When I met you, I was too scared to go down a path if I didn't know what waited at the end. But I've finally realized that no one knows what's around the next corner. It could be something wonderful, or it could be something horrible. And I realized that I don't want to go down that path without you by my side. You make the good things better and the bad things tolerable."

She started to say something, but he held up his hand.

"I know what you're going to say. Before you do, there are some things I want to give you." He handed her a key ring. "This is the key to my new truck. Well, it's new to me at least." He grinned. "It's in the parking lot. No more public transportation."

"Wow," she said. "I'm impressed."

"Just wait. There's more." He winked and handed her another key. "This is the key to my office. I started last week. I'm working for St. Jude, and I think I'm going to love it."

Her eyes widened. "You have a job *here*? In Memphis?"

He nodded and handed her a third key. "This goes to the house I'm renting in Midtown. I signed a year lease. At the end of the year, there's a possibility that I might be buying the house I grew up in."

She gestured toward a bench. "I need to sit down," she said softly.

"Of course." He followed her and took a seat next to her. He reached into his pocket and pulled out a folded-up piece of paper and handed it to her. "And now I want you to read something."

She took the paper from him. "What's this?" she asked.

"When my editor found out I was here during Elvis Week, he wanted me to do an article about it. But it kind of morphed into something else."

Suzanne unfolded the paper and met his eyes. "You didn't tell me you were writing an article about your time here."

He sighed. "I know. I didn't want to make a big deal out of it. And I really didn't want you to think I was using you just for your inside knowledge. But when you read it, you'll see that I didn't really do what Richard intended." He stood. "I have to get one more thing. I'll be right back." He hurried off in the direction of his truck. He had no idea what was going on in her head, but there was no turning back now.

❧

Suzanne could barely process things. Seeing Nick out of the blue had shocked her. She'd missed him. More than she'd realized. She opened her hand and stared at the keys he'd handed her. Nick, in Memphis with a job and a truck and a house in Midtown, seemed like some kind of mirage.

She glanced down at the article and began to read.

I grew up in Memphis but have tried for years to shake the city's dust from my boots and become a native son of anywhere else that would have me. I've lived in Atlanta and Chicago and New York. In San Diego and Barcelona and Munich. I liked to think of myself as a citizen of the world, so I spent a decade on the run, stopping only long enough to cringe if I happened to see stereotypical Memphis portrayed on TV or in movies. I distanced myself from the sports teams and the music and even the food. And in August, when a family obligation called me back to the city of my birth, I wasn't exactly enthused at having a reunion with a place I'd tried to leave firmly in my past.

As luck would have it, it was Elvis Week when I got to town, and after a conversation with my editor, I decided to write a piece poking fun at that particular tradition. But I couldn't go through with it. Because something funny happened while I was there: I fell in love with the city again, just like I had when I was a child. I uncovered the true Memphis and separated her from the cliché. Sure, there's an element that includes Elvis and barbecue and the blues. But the city is more than just that. It's the guys who turn flips on Beale Street. It's the restaurants that have been cooking the same recipes for more years than most of my readers have been alive. It's the way the barges roll by on the river just like they have for a century. It's the people who genuinely care about their neighbors and somehow manage to create a sense of small-town community within a metropolis of more than a million. It's a city that gets behind the Tigers and the Grizzlies with an intensity that surprises rival teams. And for me, a long-lost son, it's a place to call home. I came back, expecting my visit to last only a few weeks and then be over for at least another decade. Instead, I've turned in my traveling shoes for a Midtown address. And I couldn't be happier.

Suzanne looked up from the article and saw Nick walking slowly toward her, a tiny brown puppy in his arms.

"This is Presley," he said. He carefully set the puppy on the ground and clipped a leash to its collar. "Just in case you don't see enough changes in me, I figured he'd give you the complete story. I adopted him a few weeks ago, so he's not a loaner or anything." He grinned.

"He's adorable." Suzanne watched as Charlie and Presley sniffed each other. She tried to process everything that had transpired over the past few minutes, but it was difficult.

Nick bent down to untangle the puppy's leash. "I know this is a lot to take in. And I guess I could've called you weeks ago and told you what was going on. But I thought everything together might make you understand that I'm serious. I want a life here, in Memphis, and I want you to be a part of it. A big part of it."

She watched the emotions play across his face. "You never stop surprising me, do you?"

His mouth turned upward in a smile. "I hope this was a good surprise. I realize that it might be too little, too late. I knew there was a chance that you might already be with someone else." He shrugged. "But I also knew that if I didn't beg you to give us a chance, I'd never forgive myself."

She'd gone out with James a few more times, thinking she might forget Nick. But each time she'd wished she were with Nick instead and had finally told James she couldn't see him anymore. "I want to give us a chance." She smiled. "I've wanted that almost since the day I met you. I was just too scared to say it out loud." She kept a tight grip on Charlie's leash.

Nick grabbed her free hand and pulled her closer to him. "So we're going to give this a shot?" he whispered.

She nodded. "I'd like that."

Nick kissed her gently on the mouth. "I've missed you. A

lot." He grinned. "And I think Christmas in Memphis with you will be way better than Rockefeller Center or Disney."

Despite the late December chill, Suzanne felt like she was basking in warm sunshine. She'd wanted someone who was sure enough about her to take a risk. And buying a truck, accepting a job, leasing a home, and adopting a puppy were all the gestures of a man who'd clearly decided she was worth that risk.

All of a sudden, her future had no limits. She leaned forward and kissed Nick again. If he'd decided to stay a few weeks ago, it wouldn't have meant nearly as much as it did today. Today it was obvious that he'd put a lot of consideration into his decisions and that they were the result of a lot of thought and prayer, not a knee-jerk reaction.

Suzanne couldn't help but smile. Sometimes the things God had in store were so much bigger than the things she imagined for herself.

epilogue

Six months later

Suzanne glanced down at an incoming text from Avis. They were meeting for lunch today. And even though it was a bit of a drive from her east Memphis office building, Suzanne had agreed to meet Avis at Graceland.

Meet me in the chapel

Suzanne wrinkled her nose at Avis's text. She hadn't stepped foot in the chapel since her last day of work several months ago. Maybe they'd done some remodeling or something. She climbed out of her car and hurried toward the chapel. She turned the knob on the door. "Avis?" she asked as she opened the door. "Are you here?"

An Elvis song began to play softly.

Suzanne looked down the aisle and couldn't believe her eyes. Nick's dog, Presley, sat at the end of the aisle like he was about to officiate a ceremony.

She walked down the aisle and knelt down to see Presley. He'd grown a lot over the past few months and was almost as big as Charlie now. Her eyes landed on a shiny ring tied with a ribbon to Presley's collar.

"Hey," Nick said from behind her.

She turned to face him. "What are you doing here? And what is Presley doing here?" Even though the ring tied to the dog's collar gave her a pretty good idea of what they were there for, she couldn't wrap her mind around it. "I'm pretty sure it's against the rules for a dog to be here," she whispered.

Nick beamed. "I've got it on good authority that no official will be in here for at least fifteen minutes." He grinned. "Your friend Avis helped me."

Suzanne nodded. "I figured. But why?"

Nick swallowed. "Suzanne, you know I love you. I think I've loved you almost since the day we met. You shook up my life that day and rescued me from the shell of a man I was becoming."

She grinned. "I love you, too." Saying those words for the first time a few months ago had been a big step for them both, but Suzanne had never been surer of anything in her life. "And you weren't the only one who needed rescuing."

"When I met you I was a nomad, moving from one place to another, never satisfied or happy. But after I met you I began to realize what it was I was searching for all that time." He took her hands in his. "Home. I tried for ten years to find a place that felt like home to me. A place I felt safe and loved and happy. I had that once when my family was alive. But it eluded me after that. Until I met you."

Tears sprang into her eyes. "I feel the same way."

Nick dropped to one knee and untied the ring from Presley's collar. "Suzanne Simpson, you make my life brighter. You make me want to be a better person. And I want you to do me the honor of becoming my wife." He held the ring out to her. "Will you marry me?"

Even though she'd anticipated the question from the time she'd seen the diamond hanging from Presley's collar, she still gasped. "Yes. Of course," she said.

Nick stood and kissed her, first gently and then with more intensity. "I love you," he whispered as he slipped a perfect princess-cut diamond on her ring finger.

"I love you, too." She hugged him again. Today had been better than she ever could've imagined or wished for. In fact, things were so good that Suzanne knew the events were part of a bigger plan.

And knowing that made it even better.